KAIJU FALL

DOUG GOODMAN

SEVERED PRESS
HOBART TASMANIA

KAIJU FALL

WWW.SEVEREDPRESS.COM

ISBN: 978-1-925342-14-7

Texans, as I have come to know them, are an independent people. I think it comes from generations of a people who have had to fight all kinds of governments to establish their claim to the land. Perhaps that's why so many Texans pride themselves on self-sufficiency. For everyone who's had to fight off the monsters, real and unreal, just to keep a grip on that thing you call "home," this book is for you.

-2 DAYS

5:36 pm

"John Clayton Scott, get in the car," Tamara ordered her son, John Clayton. She used her Auntie voice, the one that made children stop their foolishness and come to attention like soldiers in an army. John Clayton stopped running in circles with his Lego spaceship and climbed into his seat in the mini-van. His brother, James, was already in the van, strapped into his toddler chair. James was looking at the pictures in a book that he could not read yet. Herbert the Timid Dragon. Herbert was coughing flames all over a Mercer Mayer army because Herbert was afraid. And when Herbert got afraid, he coughed.

John Clayton wished he was as easily absorbed by things as his brother. John Clayton was like his dad. He liked to build things. Legos, pinewood derby race cars, Legos, Minecraft castles, Legos. He liked to build. One day he hoped to build things like his dad. For now, though, he was content with his Nintendo DS.

On the other side of the driveway, Rylan checked the straps on the Silverado. All the straps were tight. Nothing would fall out.

He leaned over and kissed his wife through the window as she started the engine.

"I'll be right behind you," Rylan said.

"You got the checkbook?"

"Yes. I also got the drive and the sim cards."

"Everything is on the Cloud. You got the lockbox?"

"Yep."

"And we double-checked to make sure all our house information and insurance records are in the lockbox?"

"Yes."

"I think that's everything we have to have."

"Yes."

"Don't be far behind."

"I'm getting into the truck and pulling out. I'll be right behind you. I just want to check the workshop first."

"You mean the garage."

He smiled. "I mean workshop."

She kissed him again, full on the lips.

"Mom!" John Clayton groaned.

Rylan ducked out of the window, then into John Clayton's and growled at him like a bear.

"Dad, stop!" John Clayton giggled, but he liked it anyways. His dad bear-hugged him. Then he ran around the back of the minivan and jumped across James' window. James was waiting for this like a Jack in the box. When his dad finally popped out, he jumped in his seat and laughed. He got a big bear hug from his papa bear, too.

"When is Kaiju Goliad coming, Dad?" John Clayton asked.

"Not for two more days, at least."

"Is a kaiju going to smash our house?"

"Kaiju like lights, and all our lights will be out. Don't worry about it."

"I want a kaiju," James said.

"We get to visit Uncle Dre and vacation in Austin now?"

"Something like that."

Both boys erupted in cheers.

"Be good for your mom," Rylan said. "I don't want to strap any of you to the hood of the truck."

As Tamara pulled out of the driveway, she made her boys wave good-bye to their house.

7:54 pm

All evening as they drove, the relentless Texas heat came at them. The heat wavered off the highway above the long line of cars like a giant vaporous snake, a sidewinder of heat sliding up and down the highway. It made Tamara glad for air conditioning. It wasn't just the physical, almost tangible effect of the heat that bothered Tamara but the stench of it, too. Her nostrils burned with the smell of melted tar and exhaust fumes. She would need a bath when they got to her brother, Andre's, house. He had a nice new limestone off of MOPAC. Had one of those bathrooms that were as big as a small bedroom. It had a shower with two showerheads. She could get a lot of the road off of her with two showerheads.

The diaspora of cars moved at little more than a snail's pace, which was something Tamara had hoped she would never live to see. She wanted to look it up on Google, a snail's pace, wondering where the phrase came from. But she and Rylan had agreed to turn off their cell phones so they wouldn't sap the battery. Her husband said he would try to talk to her when the cars stopped, but the line never fully stopped. It moved just fast enough, maybe a turn of the wheel every minute, to prevent him from getting out of the truck and walking over to the van for a discussion on whatever. Something. Anything as long as it wasn't about kaijus. She was sick to death of kaijus. For the past week, everything was kaiju, kaiju, kaiju. Where will it land? Why was it going to Texas instead of out into the Atlantic like so many others?

Thank God for satellite radio, she thought, and turned it to her favorite station, a channel called The Groove. She liked the classics. Marvin, Stevie, and Michael. They were always good to her. They made her feel, which was important. Rylan could be an artist, but he was not fond of music. Never had been. He was fine for it for background noise, but he was just as likely to play talk radio as he was to play rock music when he was working in the garage. His phone had less than twenty songs on it when they married.

Two hours, and they had barely left the Clear Lake area. They weren't twenty minutes from their house under normal traffic conditions. That was an order of magnitude. At this rate, it would take thirty hours to get to Austin, and by then Kaiju Goliad would be bearing down on Houston.

"Mama, I want a kaiju," James said. He hadn't given up hope that one day he would have his own pet monster that stood as tall as a skyscraper.

"Well, kaiju aren't adoptable, so we can't have one."

"Why are we going to Uncle Dre's?" John Clayton asked. "Mike's family is going to a shelter in Huntsville."

"Well, we could go to a shelter in Huntsville, but we had to leave Solemnity Bay. Houston and Galveston are under mandatory evacuations."

"Mama, I gotta pee," James continued without missing a beat. John Clayton had the urge, too, but wanted Mama to know that he was holding it because he was a big boy.

"Okay."

She turned on her signal light and pulled over. Rylan followed in the Silverado. He watched John Clayton hop over James and burst into the tall roadside grass like a sprinter, then run back to the mini-van, unbuckled his brother, and then they both charged head-first into the grass, reaching for their zippers. Within seconds, the boys were trying to spell their names in urine. He chuckled, and caught his wife smiling at him in her rearview mirror.

9:02 pm

"Mama, James looks like a dead dinosaur again." James had a way of contorting his body in the car seat so that his head was arched up and back and his legs were stuck out at odd positions. When he did this, he looked like a fossilized dinosaur skeleton where the neck has craned back far enough that the dead dinosaur looks like it is trying to eat its tail.

"Get his pillow, John Clayton."

John Clayton searched the floor of the minivan for the neck pillow. He shoved it clumsily under his brother's head. He did it in such a way that it was amazing James remained asleep. But little boys can be heavy sleepers.

The sunflower yellow in the sky had gone to the great Crayola box behind the horizon, and now the lid was shut and all the world was dark except for the long train of brake lights and the faraway lights of oil factories. This was Baytown, after all, and those refineries would keep pushing until the very last moment when they were forced to shut down and stop producing money.

His dad worked at one of the plants. Tonka Oil. That wasn't it. Tanonka Oil? John Clayton wished he could remember how to pronounce the name of his dad's company. He was the oldest, so he was supposed to remember things. James wouldn't be expected to because he was too little. But John Clayton was a big boy. He was supposed to remember things like how to add multiple numbers, the water cycle, and the name of his father's company. It wasn't Tonka. Tonka was little kid's toys.

A shadow appeared off the side of the road. (Or maybe it was better to say a black form appeared because it was night, but it felt cold like a shadow.) John Clayton couldn't figure out what she shadow looked like because it stood behind tall, Southern pines. But the top of its head seemed to hover like the silhouette of a water tower in the night. This was no water tower, though. Water towers didn't move. This one moved with purpose. While the minivan crept down the highway, the shadow followed them.

He didn't want to say anything to his mama. Only little boys are afraid of the dark, and only little boys say every little doubt they have. John Clayton was expected to be more reserved. He would study the problem first, then tell his parents about it. If it really was a problem and not just his imagination running away with him.

As they snaked along the highway and out towards the Fred Hartman Bridge, John Clayton noticed little lights winking out as they passed behind the shadow. It was only then he started to get an idea of its shape. He didn't know how many arms and legs it had because they got mixed up with the trees, but he was sure it was as wide as two cars based on how long it took the lights to pass behind the shadow.

John Clayton climbed out of his seat and leaned over James so that he could get a better view.

"Son, get back in your seat," his mama yawned. She took another sip of her coffee.

"There's something out there."

"It's late and past your bedtime. You're seeing things, baby. Sit back down and try to go to sleep. Whatever it is, I'm sure it will go away."

John Clayton yawned. He was sleepy. The day had been exciting. He had been a big boy, helping his mom and dad pack for the evacuation. Sometimes he just watched his little brother. But that was a big deal, too, because James liked to wander.

John Clayton leaned back in his chair, pulled the belt buckle over his shoulder, and watched the night sky through sleep-slitted eyes. Soon he was drifting off to sleep.

He closed his eyes and listened to the gentle hum of the road. He opened his eyes one last time, just to be sure.

A red eye opened in the shadow. It was looking directly at him. Looking down at him from up above the tree line. Then a second eye, this one orange, opened and looked at John Clayton. The boy inhaled sharply and caught his breath as a stark fear wrapped around him. Two more eyes, one green and one yellow, opened on opposite sides of the head.

"Kaiju!" John Clayton yelled. When his mom didn't react, he said it over and over, pleading for his mother to solve the problem he was powerless to do anything about. "Kaiju! Kaiju! Kaiju!"

9:04 pm

The giant shape emerged from the tree line and stepped towards the line of cars. As it came towards them, Rylan did the math in his head and realized the "little" kaiju would be coming up behind the Silverado. He honked his horn at Tamara to urge her to get around other cars, even if it meant driving off the road.

He was too late, though. The cars behind him had seen the shape, too, and they were speeding down the shoulder.

Remembering that Kaiju were attracted to light, Rylan cut the engine and turned off his lights. The cars behind him did not. The monster entered the highway. Light from car headlights showed the creature to be a sinewy, toothy creature with strangely colored eyes. These were not true kaiju, though it was easily the largest animal Rylan had ever seen in his life. They were called lampreys because they followed kaiju. It was theorized that, like lampreys, they fed on the scraps that the kaiju did not eat. However, they also were known to precede kaiju falls, like they were scouting out food sources for a kaiju to make landfall. The lamprey behind his Silverado, however, seemed more intent on wanton destruction.

The lamprey grabbed the car behind Rylan and flipped it with the ease a person would flip a chair. The car crashed against another car and landed on its side. The lamprey hissed and bit another car. Its tail flung over the Silverado, and then the creature turned south towards the refinery lights and more traffic.

The long line of cars broke like a million ants suddenly breaking from their pheromone-laced line. They slammed into each other and forced their way away from the lamprey. The moving lights seemed to excite the creature more. Rylan got an idea.

He got out of the cab and climbed up to the bed, standing on the tire of his pickup. What he needed was close by and easily accessible. In that way, he was lucky. He opened a duffel bag full of his kids' favorite toys and found exactly what he was after. He set the quad copter on the ground and turned it on.

Gently, the glow-in-the-dark quad copter rose into the air. He had painted it this way because John Clayton wanted to fly it at night like an alien UFO, and Rylan, who had over-purchased for his son, did not want to lose an expensive toy that easily. So he painted it in glow-in-the-dark and tied a long glow-in-the-dark kite string to it.

The quadcopter zoomed across the lanes of traffic and over the lamprey. This was engineering on the run, literally, but if it worked, the pay-off would be tremendous.

The lamprey ignored the quad copter hovering above its four colored eyes. It was enjoying the car's shaking lights. The driver, however, had crawled to the back seat of his car to pray.

But then the lamprey did a funny thing. It glanced up, and it stared at the tiny quad copter like a kid staring at a firefly. And then it snapped its loathsome jaws at the quad copter. A little glow-in-the-dark kitestring dangled from the lamprey's mouth.

Then military copters appeared in the sky. Rylan had not heard them coming, and it was too dark to see what kind they were. They just suddenly existed, like drops of thought conjured into the sky. Missiles deployed, and machine guns chainsawed, and suddenly the quad copter-chewing lamprey was retreating back into the woods. Rylan looked down at the remote control unit in his hand. He could throw it away, but then again, that would be denying his pack rat sensibilities. He stuffed it back into the duffel bag and mentally noted the data point for future reference: kaiju follow lights.

In the dark, the lamprey fell, and the ground shook.

The little ones were easier to take down than the big ones.
The convoy continued.

ZERO DAY

Goliad was the sixth kaiju of the summer, and the first to veer towards Texas. Unlike most kaiju that ended up returning to the trench or dying in the middle of the Atlantic, Goliad curved back into the Gulf of Mexico. For five days, Rylan and Tamara watched the reports, studied the charts, and did everything they could to make sure they were ready if Goliad committed to making landfall on Houston.

On September 5, the mayor of Houston ordered the city's evacuation. Surrounding towns quickly followed. One week later, the fourth largest city in the United States was a ghost town.

On September 13, Goliad came ashore…

7:22 pm

Rylan and Tamara and the whole world got to watch Goliad's destruction first-hand thanks to a small army of cameras set up on tower rooftops and at strategic vantage points throughout the area. Rylan and Tamara held hands while they watched the television show shots of the vacated boardwalk, not two miles from their home. At first the cameras showed nothing. It was early evening, the kind that seems perfect in Houston. Great sweeping clouds filled the sky. The sun was streaming gold everywhere. It was a night for football and romance. Except tonight there would be no Friday night lights.

What most people noticed first was the wildlife. Some of the streets closest to the bay looked like those tiny Pacific islands that get overrun with mating crabs. But the blue crabs invading Clear Lake were not participating in some ancient reproductive ritual. Ancient, evolutionary mechanisms in the crab had warned them to escape the presence of the kaiju lurking in the bay.

So, too, the fish of the sea were trying to escape. From drone footage looking down on the bay, it seemed like the bay was host to some Cthulhu monster with shadowy tentacles radiating out to the coastline. These tentacles were nothing so nefarious. They were schools of fish seeking refuge from the titan waiting in the ship channel.

The scientists who studied kaiju were predicting that Goliad would wait until nightfall to leave the bay. Like so many trench species, kaiju preferred the dark. (Though they were attracted to little lights, Rylan remembered.) Goliad waited, partially submerged in a shipping channel.

His armored back stayed above water, looking like an island or a floating continent covered in wicked, spiked trees that seemed pulled from angles unknown to physics. The military took the opportunity to convince Goliad to leave by laying down controlled missile fire. For a moment, it seemed like it would work. Goliad pulled away from the shoreline.

First, the coast shimmered. This was the light reflecting off the scales of fish as they fled the kaiju. Just before the kaiju moved, the same Darwinian mechanisms that told the blue crabs to flee, told the fish of the sea to escape. The coastline seethed.

Then the tide surged forward, pushing ashore like a thousand battering rams that leveled homes and flooded properties. Palm trees fell like matchsticks when a hurricane blows through.

A giant mass lunged out of the water. The camera atop of the boardwalk Ferris wheel caught the rise of the titan on film. Mass and sea foam rose up to block the sky. Then Goliad moved, a dark appendage that struck the amusement park ride. Camera and Ferris wheel fell downward as the monster continued to rise up out of the bay.

Tamara white-knuckled Rylan's fist. She hadn't gripped his hand this tightly since John Clayton's birth.

Goliad was one of the largest kaiju ever to make landfall. By classification, he was officially daikaiju, a super-sized monster. He was so gigantic, he was picked up on Doppler radar. The creature looked like a giant wolverine. An armored, eight-legged black wolverine covered in slick scales. And just like a wolverine, the first thing Goliad did was attack a Comanche helicopter like it was anything but a gnat to the five-mile long creature. Gunfire lit up the evening sky, missiles deployed, and Goliad bit down on an A-10 Warthog.

Each kaiju was different, so the military rarely knew how to respond until the kaiju first appeared. Goliad was covered on top by impregnable armor plates. Not even the deadliest ballistic missiles made a dent.

The kaiju headed north, out of the bay. He made landfall north of LaPorte, then moved toward the city and the port. The Port of Houston is one of the biggest ports in the nation, and it is encircled by some of the largest oil refineries in the world. The catastrophic effect to the world's market and the economy had been one of the major bullet points of talking heads for the past week. No way was Uncle Sam taking a chance, though. A line had been drawn in the sand on highway 225, not two hundred yards from the Battle of San Jacinto marker where Sam Houston had cried out "Remember the Alamo!"

When Goliad crossed that line, the monster found five thousand troops supported by some of the greatest artillery known in the history of the world. The weaponry had specifically been redesigned to attack kaiju. Gunmen fired with armor piercing bullets, and tanks thundered their opposition to Goliad's advance. Goliad roared, but his roar was cut off by the sound of armor-piercing bullets exploding inside him. He was weakest where he was hardest to reach, low under the belly. The kaiju shook and stumbled on one leg. Pits appeared on his underbelly. Hit by such relentless firepower, a bloody Goliad finally turned from his path, but not before taking out most of the forces by turning and sweeping his blunted tail across the state road they had used as their line in the sand.

A-10s and Comanche helicopters followed him, trying to convince him to go back out to the bay. Goliad retreated back into South Houston. From their televisions and their phones, people smiled, cheered, and high-fived. An announcer wiped tears. This could have gone really badly. Most did. People talked about New Orleans and Key West and how much improved the response was. But in Austin, Rylan and Tamara watched Goliad's direction of travel with increasing concern. They prayed he didn't go back toward Solemnity Bay, where they lived.

Goliad refused to go east back into the bay. Maybe it was the wolverine in him, but he still wanted to fight. He jumped and leapt at A-10s and Apaches as they dive-bombed him like angry mockingbirds protecting their nests. His path led him south through a patch-quilt of swamps, bayous, and suburban neighborhoods. As the sun disappeared on a horizon that only Goliad and the jet fighters could see, the Johnson Space Center loomed before him. Goliad roared into the fading light, and as his head appeared over the tree line, a new troop of soldiers barraged him with gunfire and RPGs. This group was fewer in number than the soldiers defending the refineries and port, with only a dozen tanks.

Goliad lowered his body to make it harder to hit him, then he charged the soldiers, his mouth open and his eight legs stomping like pistons. Goliad went berserk, attacking each tank single-handedly, ensuring that each tank was not just destroyed, but smashed, obliterated, and devoured before moving to the next tank.

A self-sacrificing pilot took the God-given slim chance to attack Goliad's underbelly while the monster was distracted by his own gluttonous savagery. It was an instantaneous reaction to a window of opportunity that the pilot knew would not be there again if she radioed in her plan. This was war, though, so superiors would have to understand. The pilot steered her Warthog between two stomping legs. The A-10 rolled as it passed between the monster's legs. Gunfire stopped. The underbelly of the beast appeared. The pilot shot all the Warthog's remaining Tomahawks and strafed the monster's underside. The effect was as if a knife had cut through the monster's skin.

Goliad reacted immediately, dropping to the ground, then jumping and spinning. As the monster landed, he created a shockwave that flipped nearby cars and hurled soldiers fifty feet into the air. The baleful roar that came from the monster filled the air with sound. Like all the oxygen in the air had been replaced with tangible sound.

Goliad left a river of blood as he retreated back toward the bay. He crashed through the NASA causeway and fell once into Clear Lake.

"That's the best place for him," Tamara's brother said. "If he doesn't try to make it out to the bay. Then he'll go through Solemnity Bay."

"Shut up!" Tamara and Rylan yelled simultaneously.

While A-10s and Apaches pursued him, he clawed his way across the lake, then turned in front of the Solemnity Bay Bridge. He stared sickly at the helicopters that hovered around him. They ceased fire and waited for the inevitable. Goliad no longer had the strength to attack.

Goliad cantered on his side, then fell dead on his back. When the smoke cleared, he lay like a mountain in the skyline. His head lay in one county, his tail in another. The last fiery rays of the sun alighted on his claws.

He fell in Solemnity Bay.

"NOOOOO!!!" Rylan screamed at the television set.

More than 60 years of growth and development was reduced to razed apocalypse.

45 minutes had passed.

+9 DAYS

2:00 pm

From above a ribbon of stock market prices, weather updates, and major headlines, the CNN newscaster said, "What Goliad decimated in less than an hour took nine days before people could begin returning to their homes and putting their lives back together. Before residents could return, FEMA had to determine the area was clear and safe. The Army Corps of Engineers conducted studies on Goliad's corpse to determine if his body would shift after death, especially if it would curve and destroy more homes. Before the Army Corps of Engineers could enter the area, though, the CDC, working in conjunction with FEMA, determined the amount of gassing and the levels of toxic fumes that would enter the area due to Goliad's decomposing. Until the CDC, Army Corps of Engineers, and FEMA assessments were complete, all emergency responders were required to wear hazmat suits and stay away from the corpse.

Once the engineers decided that the corpse wasn't going to adjust in his death stance, and once the air around Goliad was deemed safe from toxins, the process began for preparing the area so that residents could return to their homes. Most people will be able to return to their homes permanently, but areas of high damage such as those near the Kaiju fall must wait longer so that the government can ensure their safe return, even if just long enough so home owners can assess the damage to their property."

The program cut from the newscaster to an interview of Dr. John Garrido, the Goliad lead commander from NOAA's Kaiju Services branch. Dr. Garrido, in blue jeans, cowboy boots, and a dirty polo shirt, was a stark contrast to the crisp look of the newscaster. Dr. Garrido said, "This is a multi-departmental response. DOD handles Kaiju prevention. NOAA and FEMA work on dismantling and studying the corpse while, with the CDC and Army Corps of Engineers, ensuring the safe return of American residents."

"And what is preventing that return?" an off-camera interviewer asked.

"First of all, some residents are able to return. But in the areas surrounding the kaiju fall, we have serious issues. There is no water, no electricity, no sewage, no medical care, and a daikaiju corpse decomposing in people's backyards."

"Is this a militarized zone?" the off camera interviewer asked.

Dr. Garrido glared at him for a second, his best Clint Eastwood impersonation, then responded. "This is a quarantine zone, not a militarized zone, with jurisdiction to NOAA."

"What is preventing residents from returning, or looters from looting?"

"As in all kaiju responses, we have enlisted the help of local law enforcement as well as state troopers, who will monitor the roads to prevent looting."

"Do you have any message for the people who want to return their homes?"

Dr. Garrido looked at the camera. "Stay where you are. Let us finish our job, and when the time is appropriate and safe, we will begin the permanent return to the Clear Lake area. In the meantime, monitor your news, hug your neighbors, and we will begin a phased, temporary return for residents to assess damages."

Rylan turned off the TV set and looked at his reflection in the slick, blackened mirror. It looked like a shadow had fallen over him, even though he was standing in the middle of a room in daylight with all the curtains pulled back. Behind him, he saw the reflections of his wife and children, who sat in the light. Tamara was reading to them. Baby Tarzan, of course.

"It's just the news. They're paid to sensationalize, so whatever you're thinking, stop thinking about it."

"I was thinking of my father. When I was a kid, our house was hit by a tornado, but he built it back, every last brick, and better than before. He added a sunroom for my mom."

"That's my kind of room."

"Mommy, read the story!"

"Oh, I'm sorry. Baby Tarzan likes to jump on trees. Baby Tarzan likes to swing from the vines…"

While Baby Tarzan swam with the elephants, Rylan thought about his house and wondered if he had what it took to rebuild it brick-by-brick.

+10 Days

2:00 am

For Rylan, the tenth day after the kaiju fall began on the road from Austin. Kisses from his boys John Clayton and James Howlett and his wife Tamara. They had evacuated to her brother Andre's, and now they were staying with him, sleeping on couches and hide-away beds until they were allowed to return home.

"Be careful," Tamara told him. Her hands, colored like Houston clay, were tethered to his jeans by the tips of her nail-bitten fingers. "If they tell you to leave, leave."

"I'm getting home today one way or another."

"Home is where your family is." She kissed him long until James started begging to go back to bed. She picked up James. Rylan opened up the pickup's door, and John Clayton ran up and gripped his leg.

"I'll be back soon, John Clayton."

There were tears in his eyes.

"Why are you crying?"

"Don't let the monsters get you, Daddy."

"There aren't any monsters there anymore. Your old man's coming back. In the meantime, you can play with your cousins."

"I don't want to play with my cousins."

"Why?"

"Jordan plays stupid video games."

Rylan suppressed a laugh. He looked at Tamara and said, "Well, Mommy will make sure you and Jordan only play cool video games, okay?"

"Okay."

Rylan lifted his four year old and placed him, too, in Tamara's other arm.

"I wish it was different," he said.

"Don't be," she said. "We'll be okay. Be careful on the road."

1:45 pm

Rylan gripped the steering wheel. It was brutal hot in Texas again, and the humidity clung to everything, making his clothes, the steering wheel, and even the air sticky. Turning the air conditioner on his old four-wheel drive full blast did little to keep the heat at bay.

Rylan waited in a car lane that clogged the interstate like the artery of a giant about to have a colossal heart attack. Thousands of cars waited to be allowed back into the Clear Lake area so that homeowners could assess their damaged homes and snap photos for insurance companies. They could end the speculation of whether or not their home was salvageable.

FEMA and DPS were out in full force, directing traffic, verifying licenses, and handing out pamphlets with instructions for the day. Helicopters hovered overhead. Some were from the local Houston affiliates. Others were police choppers there to remind everybody of the consequences of not waiting patiently.

Goliad lay ten days dead on the coast. His corpse was visible all the way from the interstate overpasses in downtown Houston. As Rylan drove through the downtown area, he was shocked at the sheer size of Goliad. He had watched Goliad's ascent from the bay and his destruction of south Houston. He had seen it replayed over and over again while he and his wife tried to figure out whether Goliad had landed on their house. (An hour-long wait on a special hotline proved that their house was not a confirmed loss, and confirmed them for the return visit.) But the magnitude of the kaiju's size did not hit him until he saw Goliad's feet up in the air, jutting from the coast like mountain peaks.

He arrived before dawn and had to wait more than half the day before he was allowed to enter Clear Lake. Day 10 was the second day allotted for people from specially designated zones to return to their homes for damage assessment. Day 10 was Zone 2, which included parts of the coast in Galveston County, including Solemnity Bay, Baycliff, and South Shore. The previous day, the first people were allowed to assess damage, were residents of Seabrook, El Lago, and parts of South Houston.

By 2pm, he was waiting for clearance when the troopers came out with megaphones. They fanned out across the lanes. The trooper in Rylan's lane stood in front of his bumper, raised the megaphone, and announced, "No vehicles will be admitted beyond me. There is a backlog from yesterday's Zone 1 entrants. Return home and watch the news for further direction about when this zone re-opens."

A chorus of disgruntled curses and honking horns countered the announcement.

Rylan cursed his bad fortune. Then he noticed that the troopers in the other lanes were standing farther up the road and behind him. "Hey, what about me? The other troopers are back there." The trooper looked at the other lanes, then walked behind Rylan and repeated the announcement.

Thirty minutes later, Rylan handed his license over to the trooper in front of the barricade. He showed his license and his allergen mask. "Remember, be out by nightfall," the trooper said, handing him a pamphlet and raising the barricade for Rylan to pass.

This was the easy part. The tough part would be evading the police until his house was fixed back up for his family.

Once past the barricade, his was the only car on the road. The power was out, so all the intersections were stop signs.

Rylan was still amazed at Goliad's size. This was truly a Texas-sized daikaiju. Every time he thought the monster couldn't possibly get any larger, he drove closer to the coast and the monster grew higher into the sky. Hundreds of gulls perched and flocked around Goliad. Every flying scavenger from the Texas Gulf Coast seemed to be roosting on Goliad. Pipers, pelicans, grackles, and even raptors were all feasting on the carcass. It was speculated that if left alone, a kaiju would feed the world for a hundred years.

Rylan was hopeful. There was debris on the streets, but nothing too major. A few holes in houses, probably caused by debris thrown up by Goliad's fall. The streetlights and telephone poles were angled all in one direction away from the blast. Overall, nothing looked too damaged.

The detour sign hung almost limply on the edge of Goliad's footprint. It was at least twenty yards across and five feet deep. The road, the sidewalk, and half the houses in the area were squashed or knocked over. All the houses in at least a hundred yard radius had suffered severe damage. A crying woman kneeled in her front yard as if praying for God to do something about the mess of bricks and siding that used to be her home. Then he got a feeling in his gut, like his stomach lining was being torn off in strips and leaving nothing there to hold in his acid. He shifted in the seat.

Against his will (the trick to escaping Gozer is to empty your mind, but Dan Aykroyd always thought of Mr. Stay Puft, didn't he?), Rylan thought of his family coming out of the basement after the tornado and finding nothing but bricks and boards. Gone was the dining room, the kitchen, and the bedrooms. No coffee table family heirloom, no Nintendo, no science fair ribbons. There was a Volkswagen Bug in the area that used to be the bathroom. It was a Baja Bug with the modified engine, off-road tires, and hood removed from the back of the car. It was also about half its original size because it looked like some mad Lovecraftian god had slammed it down on the ground. Half the front was crumpled, and the Bug was now sitting on its top.

Off to the side of what used to be the house, there was a deer, or what looked like a deer, in one of the piles of bricks.

"Stay away from there," his mother had admonished him. But she was too taken aback by the absolute pulverization of their neighborhood to make him stop.

"I'll be careful," little Rylan said as he walked up to the brown pelt in the bricks, curious of death like all children. He reached out and put his hand on the brown pelt, then stroked it. The fur felt smooth under his fingertips. Soft he had expected, but not so smooth. He thought it would feel more like a cow. Deer was slicker. All these years later, he still remembered the touch of the deer in his hands. Perhaps because of what came next.

The skin jerked away from him, and a tall deer (at least tall for a nine-year old) rose up out of the bricks. It was like a dragon from those mall shops that sell metal dragons that look like they are emerging from the rock they are cast in. The deer seemed born of brick and mortar. As it shook off the mortar dust, Rylan's mother harshly whispered to him to stay still and not make a move. Rylan did as his mother told. The deer looked down at Rylan, as perplexed as Rylan was, if not more confused. And then it ran away.

Rylan followed the detour around the footprint and back onto the main road. Ten minutes later, the familiar blue color of his subdivision's walls appeared. Dolphin Cove. His home, or at least, he hoped, what was left of his home. Strung up along the side of the subdivision wall was a giant Come and Take It flag, cut up by flying debris. Over the canon, somebody had painted a resemblance of Kaiju Goliad. Rylan couldn't remember who made the flag, but he remembered seeing it before he left. And he had never felt so relieved as when he first saw its picture on the news.

Above the flag, the corpse swelled outward. In the early afternoon, this close to the kaiju, the sun had been up over the body less than an hour.

Entering the subdivision, Rylan regripped the steering wheel. With the images of the footprint and the crying woman swirling in his mind with images of deer rising out of bricks, he, too, said a hundred little prayers that his house would still be standing. That the Big Bad Wolf hadn't blown it down like a house of straw. He was not encouraged by the row of destruction to his left. The houses closest to Goliad were desolation. Nor was he encouraged by all the debris lying in the street. Most of it had been pushed aside, presumably by government workers when they were clearing the area for people to return. Long post beams and a restaurant sign declaring "KAIJU NIGHT $3 MARGARITAS" were pushed to the side of the street. A giant blood stain was smeared across the road. Rylan followed the stain through the grass, over a driveway, and covering half a house. It had already been spray-washed by chemicals, but the stain had sunk into the siding the way bloodstains settle into pores and creases.

The stop sign at the intersection was on its side. Rylan said another prayer and turned right. His house was the corner house facing Goliad. Either it was there or it wasn't. He said another prayer.

His heart leaped with joy to see his two-story still intact. Some of his gutters were down, there was a hole in his roof, and most of his fence was down, but otherwise, his house was still standing. He parked his truck in the driveway and pulled out the video camera.

Dust and rocks from Goliad's fall had settled everywhere. Rylan put his allergen mask on. As he stepped across his lawn, which thankfully was devoid of giant blood stains, his boots made footprints in the dust. Using his phone, he filmed a panorama of the front yard, showing the sticks fallen from his oak tree and the shingles from the roof. A gutter clung to the siding like an action star with nothing but a few fingertips keeping him from falling to his death. Another gutter was completely gone. Rylan looked down the side street, in his neighbor's yards. It was as if the gutter had vanished or been teleported away by aliens. Maybe it was in Galveston, for all he knew. Three-fourths of his fence line was toppled over, barely missing his palm tree. His peppers, jalapenos for him and bell for the family, however, had suffered the brunt of the fence line's trauma. Small chunks of siding were ripped off of the walls.

He remembered putting the peppers in. Tamara had bought him Houston Dynamo work gloves, and little gloves for his two sons. She filmed the three of them digging in the dirt together.

"What are peppers, Daddy?" John Clayton had asked.

"They are something you can eat with just about anything, and they cost almost half a dollar at the store, so hopefully this should save us a few dollars."

He helped them smooth out the hole where they would plug the pepper plants. Three green peppers and one jalapeno.

"Can you eat them with chicken nuggets?"

"Sure, you can."

"I like chicken nuggets."

"Everybody likes chicken nuggets."

"Except mommy!" Tamara barked from behind the camera. "Mommy likes steak!"

"Steak is great," John Clayton recited.

"Steak is great," Rylan laughed. Then he plugged the holes with pepper plants.

"Now this last one is exceptionally good. You can put it in chili, or you can sauté it with other vegetables for a little kick, or you can do what Daddy likes to do, and wrap it in bacon and grill it."

"That's gross!" John Clayton declared. James Howlett agreed, saying "Goss, Goss, Goss."

"He's a son after your liking," Rylan said to Tamara.

"Are you kidding? Momma likes a little spice, you should know that."

It was going to be a good grilling season.

Rylan tallied the damage in his head, keeping in mind what was salvageable before his family returned. The holes in his siding did not go all the way through. He could bandage them with tarps until he got somebody to put in new siding. The busted windows he could replace, and the fence he could get started on tonight if he wanted.

Inside, water damage was the problem. With a broken window, rains had damaged his sofas and about half the carpet. The smell of rot and funk filled his nose. Leaves and twigs had blown in, too. Hadn't it been a bit like that when they bought it foreclosed? Leaves, plumbing issues, some rot? Add some spray-painted anti-establishment manifestos against mom and dad, and this could be the same house less than five years ago.

Upstairs he found more leaves.

"Shit."

John Clayton's room was ruined. The ceiling sunk and opened, exposing insulation that hung in the air like the intestines of a very large and very pink monster. John Clayton's bed absorbed the brunt of the rain, but his dresser was knocked over, and his carpet would have to be replaced, too.

The entrance to the Secret Room loomed over him. A ray of light shined down, giving Rylan a sinking feeling.

Camera in one hand, he steadily climbed into the hole in the ceiling. Upstairs, the small room was full of stuffed animals, play sets, and little toy cars. There was a dresser against the back corner, and there was another hole on the adjacent side. This was James Howlett's entrance to the Secret Room.

Most parents buy cribs and paint the baby room. Rylan built rooms where his sons could play alone and keep all their toys. It took him weeks to design and build the ventilation system, add extra insulation, and put in the sidewalls. But when he finished, his sons had "the coolest bedroom in Solemnity Bay" according to their friends.

The stench was overpowering. The hole in the roof was at least five feet in diameter. Three rafters would have to be completely replaced along with the plywood rooftop, the ridge vents, and the shingles.

Something large and feral jumped up and out of the hole.

"What the?"

He stumbled and nearly fell back down out of the Secret Place. Lost the camera and had to retrieve it. Then he let his heartbeat go down from about a thousand beats a minute and caught his breath. His mind raced through every animal he could think of. Maybe it was a large skunk or a very dark bobcat. But if he was being honest, he would have compared it to a chimpanzee/black panther hybrid thing. It must have been a large skunk.

In its place, he saw a giant organ, or maybe just a piece of an organ. He wasn't familiar with kaiju anatomy, and since no kaiju had been classified as the same species, Rylan doubted there was anyone who could tell him what he was looking at. Whatever it was, it was bulbous and nauseating, with thick, flat arteries like banana veins from its skin after being peeled. The arteries extended to the floor. He zoomed the camera on the organ. He started thinking of how to remove it from his property. Couldn't think of anything that would work that wasn't a crane, so he decided to look into rubber gloves and bleach.

4:00 pm

"Hey, babe."

"You got in? I heard that a lot of people were denied."

"Yeah. Just made it. I'm home."

"And?"

"We still have a home."

"YES!"

"I will try to send you photos if I can. We don't have electricity yet. A couple missing gutters, the fence, a broken window. We will have to replace some carpet. So we're okay. How are the boys?"

"They are good. And even if they were bad, hon, I don't care. WE HAVE A HOUSE!" Rylan heard his brother-in-law cheering in the background.

"Okay, I need to let you go."

"Don't ever let me go."

"You know what I mean. Low battery. I've got a lot of work to do."

"You were on the road all day, Rylan. And you've accomplished the first goal: we have a house. Get some rest."

"Nice one. How many lines of code you write today?"

"Hush."

"Teleworking has its perks."

"Be careful."

"Okay."

"I mean it. Do you remember the last time I told you to be careful?"

"A week ago in the shop?"

"Try a month ago when you were helping some idiot fly a lawnmower."

"Parasail, and the mods worked mostly perfectly."

Tamara sighed. "I love you."

"Love you, too."

He hung up. He wasn't sure why he didn't tell her about the giant hole in the roof, the chunk of Goliad in the Secret Room, or the thing that climbed out. Maybe it was his pride. Maybe he didn't want to admit to her that there were things he couldn't take care of. Things more dangerous than parasailing over coastal plains. Or maybe he just didn't want to acknowledge that he had no friggin idea what he was dealing with.

To air out his mildew-smelling house, he removed plywood from half his windows and opened all the ones that weren't broken, then decided he, too, needed air that didn't hover around seventy or eighty percent humidity.

Outside, he saw Lisa and Ainsley across the street. They lived in one of the nicest homes in the subdivision, though the Homeowner's Association was always coming down on them for not painting it in the preferred neutral colors. Lisa was a playwright or an artist, so it was no shock when she started to use the house as another artistic outlet. But to the HOA, mango and avocado were foods to eat, not colors to paint on the outside of a house.

Ainsley was shoveling shingles into the garbage bin. She looked no dirtier than usual, meaning she was covered in dust. (As a biologist from Galveston, she often came home covered in mud and ticks and smelling like dead animals.") Lisa was washing the windows. Their boards were already neatly stacked in the garage as if they had never been bolted to siding. Ainsley waved, and Rylan waved back.

"You make it okay?" he asked as he walked up. They hugged.

"The Bradford in the backyard took the brunt of the damage. Now I'm just concerned about Goliad's corpse. If he leans our way as people claim, none of this is worth anything. Lisa swears it's leaning towards us. How about you? You're the engineer. Do you think it will fall this way?"

"I think it will continue to sink into the ground and stay where it is until calcium miners get to it, and then it will be turned into a tourist attraction. Goliad World or something."

Lisa decided she had washed enough windows and came over. "Your house looks good, Rylan."

"I have a five-foot hole in the roof."

"How deep is the damage?"

"John Clayton's bed took most of it. It's mostly leaves and dirt that blew in when Goliad crashed. There was something unusual, though. I went up there, into their Secret Rooms, and there was this thing."

"What kind of thing?" It was Jim Dao, an old man with a body as tight as a fishing line with a Marlin fighting on the other end. He and his wife Christine were an elderly Vietnamese family who lived two houses down from Rylan. Jim supervised a small fleet of shrimping boats.

"Want to come look?"

6:00 pm

The five stood around the organ while humidity sank into the Secret Room from the hole in the roof. The heat of the world seemed to be trapped there. Even Jim, who had spent many years out in the bay hauling nets in the summertime, even he wiped away sweat from his weather-beaten brow.

"What is it?" Lisa asked as she tucked her arm around Ainsley's.

"It must have come off Goliad before he died. What exactly it is, though, is beyond me. What do you think, Ainsley?"

"I think you should report this to FEMA. You don't know if it's dangerous."

"But what if it's just a piece of meat?"

"A piece of meat from what? We know very little about the kaiju. I mean, they are coming ashore to die, like beached whales, but not like beached whales. They come angry and destructive and then they fall down and die. You know kaiju fall is taken from whale fall, which is when a whale dies and sinks to the bottom of the ocean and every kind of sea creature from crabs to sharks comes to get in line at the buffet. It's kind of funny when you think of it. Kaiju is a portmanteau of the words for gorilla and whale. But we don't know what caused the kaiju's death. Was Goliad sick? Was his navigation system in his head messed up? Did it have something to do with pressure imbalance? And now that he is here, is he covered in toxins and parasites, or what? You should report this and get it removed from your house."

Jim nodded his agreement with Ainsley. "I've pulled up lots of fish from the sea. Some are rotten and some are dangerous. You should call someone."

"Or," Lisa interjected, "just playing devil's advocate here and not trying to contradict or undermine my beloved in any way: you can wait and see. It isn't doing anything to you or the house up here. And if you tell FEMA, they are going to kick you out of the Cove, that's for certain."

"So wait, see if anything happens, fix up the house, and then if I can't get rid of it my own self, call the authorities then?"

Lisa nodded. Ainsley shrugged. Jim exhaled his disagreement. He leaned down and, against his wife's protest, placed his open hand on the organ. He closed his eyes and listened to the organ.

"Have you considered that it is an egg?" he asked, his voice steady as the ocean after a storm.

"No. Maybe."

Rylan put his hand on the organ, but he didn't feel whatever Jim was sensing.

"I think it is an egg. Something is inside. It must be an embryo."

"Are you sure?"

"Look, maybe you are going about this all wrong," Ainsley said. "Maybe you should call NOAA. They could come in here, remove this egg-thing, and study it."

"I call NOAA or FEMA, the end result is the same. Me out of the house. Hell, they may decide it is better to study the thing in my house, and then where do I live?"

Jim shrugged. "Call FEMA. Call NOAA. If you don't want to call them, then kill it. Stab it with an iron or a shovel, but make sure it is dead."

Jim let go of the egg and started down the ladder.

"Call FEMA or kill it!" he said as he and his wife disappeared, returning to their home.

"Assuming it's alive," Rylan called down after them.

Ainsley took a few photos with her cell phone. "Do you mind? I just want to ponder this one a bit."

While Ainsley shot pictures, Lisa said, "It's your call, Rylan. Your house, your rules."

"But you wouldn't do it."

"I didn't say that. I said, 'playing devil's advocate.' I trust Ainsley. If she told me to piss on it until the authorities came cause that has some kind of biological function, I'd do it. But that's me. You've got to decide."

"You're an odd person."

"I create living sculptures for a living. Then again, I never got in a shark cage."

"That was one time a long time ago."

Lisa chuckled.

"I don't want to leave my house."

"I get that. We've seen what happens after kaiju attacks. It's like hurricanes, sometimes. People go a little crazy. Looters show up. I've watched reports about gangs targeting some of the suburbs. They sweep in one night, quiet as a mouse, and steal all the goods while everybody's gone. You think I'm going to let some gangbanger steal everything I've worked to make my own? I'm going to put up a sign out front that says, "Navy Sniper.""

"You weren't a sniper."

"They don't know that."

The Secret Room was too hot to stay inside, so after Ainsley and Lisa left, Rylan shut the door to the Secret Room. He pulled his truck into the garage and closed the door. This was his sanctuary. Just the smell alone calmed him: a combination of a well-cleaned room that can't wipe out the faint trace of oil and grime. It was like the thin collection of black under the fingernails that signified dedication and innovation, two things he prided himself in.

It wasn't a man cave, which he felt was a euphemism for excess. Rylan wasn't worshiping at the altar of sports and entertainment, and he wasn't showing off his love of trashy décor or log cabins or busty women. There was no beer-bottle clock on the wall. This was his workshop, where he got things done and made things happen. In here, he had installed the Silverado's rockers. He had created a laser for turning off the streetlamp so he could stargaze with his kids. He built the air duct system for the Secret Room. And yes, he had modified a parasail for a friend and completed a few other fun projects. But it was all accomplishment. Not glorification.

Tamara had wanted to get a sign like the one from the old Discovery Channel show, Monster Garage. Eventually, he blowtorched "Hiawatha's Garage" on a metal plate and hung it on the wall. It was an inside joke.

All the equipment had been lifted onto counters just in case water surged into the workshop. Rylan took care into returning the various welding, grinding, lifting, and compressing mechanisms to their rightful place. Then he unloaded the generator and gas cans. He left the fence posts in the truck bed.

Once he finished in the workshop, he moved into the house-proper and began moving furniture downstairs and cutting up the carpet, which he rolled up and pushed aside.

Like a house cat with a full belly, evening took its time rolling into Dolphin's Cove. Rylan cracked a Shiner, leaned into his couch, and rested. He must have fallen asleep because the next thing he heard sounded like somebody pummeling his front door. Red and blue lights flashed through the broken windowpanes.

"Mr. Scott?" an officer said. Rylan heard the officer clearly; his voice boomed through the open windows. The police officer waited a moment, then knocked on the door again. Rylan stayed glued to his couch and hoped the police officer couldn't look through the windows.

"Mr. Scott? If you're still in there, this is a restricted zone by authority of NOAA. One-day passes were allowed with the caveat that you would be out by sundown. This is your last warning. If you are found on the premises or in the zone after sundown, you will be removed forcefully from the subdivsion and arrested if necessary. This is a dangerous area that has not been fully cleared by FEMA or Kaiju Services. You need to leave immediately."

After a moment, he heard footsteps walking away down his front walkway. The officer at the door said to another officer, "Must have left without being signed out."

"Well, either that, or he's going to be breaking the law," the other officer said. The second officer had a dour, *I'm too old for this shit*, voice. Car doors shut. The red and blue lights moved a little farther down the street.

Rylan walked upstairs and peaked through the blinds out of the window of his bedroom. He saw the officers, two men in their mid-twenties, walking up the sidewalk to his next-door neighbor's house. The officer banged on that door, too, while the other waited at the curb. The second officer, who had huge bags under his eyes and bad facial shadow (he really did look like he felt too old for this shit) glanced up at Rylan's house and at the window Rylan was peering out from. Rylan retreated to his bed and waited for the officers to return to his house and force him out. When they didn't, he fell back asleep.

+11 DAYS

4:00 am

Something crashed outside, jostling him from his sleep. He pulled on his working boots and went to the blinds and scanned the street. Without any power, it was difficult to make anything out. The blackness felt as thick as the humidity. He grabbed the flashlight from his side table, laced up his boots, and walked downstairs and out the front door.

He was taken aback by the lack of human noise. No cars, no electric hums of streetlights, no dogs barking in the night. It was peaceful.

Directly across the street from him, his neighbor had spray-painted "Trespassers Will Be Shot Looters Will Be Shot Dead" over the plywood covering his windows. Rylan guessed that Ainsley and Lisa weren't the only ones anticipating thieves and looters.

Hearing movement, he shined his light on the pile of garbage and debris in his neighbor's lawn. A raccoon looked at him casually, then returned to his scavenging.

"You didn't make that crash," Rylan said. He shined his light back down the dark cul-de-sac. His light caused shadow fingers to dance behind trees. He imagined a giant hooded figure, like a grim reaper without the sickle, standing in the middle of the street watching him.

On a whim, he shined the beam up into the sky. His flashlight was hopelessly ill-suited for reaching the top of Goliad's carcass. He could see the monster's shape, though. The top of his large spine was like a black silhouette against the night sky. Over the tips of Goliad's ribs, the Milky Way exploded. With little to no lights in the area, the Milky Way took center stage in the night sky in a way that hadn't been seen in decades. Small shadows flew overhead. He wondered what kinds of birds were flocking to the carcass now. Were they new birds, or were there bellies plump with kaiju flesh? He heard some crying out to each other, and guessed that grackles or seagulls were nearby.

He waved his flashlight in the air like it was a lightsaber. Even made the movie projector sounds. Twirled in the middle of the street and crouched down, slashing the beam of his flashlight on the ground. Skywalkers had nothing on him. Then he stopped.

He definitely had the feeling that something or someone was watching him again. He panned his light across the open intersection. The beam was heavy with humidity. Something was out there. He could sense it. Was it a looter? A scout from a gang looking for places to rob?

He waited long enough to feel a bead of sweat throb down his temple like a fat thumb. Then he made the sound again. It was the sound of all that was good in the world, the sound of strength. He backed up, flipped the flashlight-saber in his hand, then did another twirling move to fight back the darkness.

His beam landed on the bloody face of a mountain lion.

Rylan dropped the flashlight, then picked it up again and aimed it at the lion's eyes reflecting green. The mountain lion paused to consider Rylan, licking his flat tongue against his blood-soaked mouth. His belly was distended. Bloated with blood and God knew what else. Rylan froze. The mountain lion's tail twitched. Rylan didn't move. Didn't make a sound. His mind flooded with potential scenarios, most ending with him being dragged by a mountain lion. (Maybe he could make it to the front door of his house, if he left it unlocked. Had he left it unlocked?) These thoughts shot through him fast as molecules in a Hadron Collider. Then, the mountain lion walked off down the street as leisurely as if he were considering buying property in the neighborhood.

Rylan did not move as he watched the mountain lion submerge back into the night from which it came. Mountain lions had been sighted before, but never this close to neighborhoods. They stayed to the state parks and the outskirts of towns that lay dozens of miles from here. Never had he heard of a mountain lion being seen this close to the bay, or even this side of the interstate.

He looked back up to the dark void that was Goliad's silhouette. He should have known that a kaiju fall this large would attract all kinds of scavengers. What other predators would smell the blood in the air and come looking for a free meal? Coyotes? Gators? Bears? Bears hadn't been seen in southeast Texas in over a hundred years, though if there was ever something to bring them out, this would be it. He made a mental note to visit the kaiju fall later in the day.

Another crash as strong as the first one that woke him reverberated in the hot silence of the night. It sounded like wood or old sheet metal crashing. This time, Rylan was able to determine the direction of the sound. He ran towards the intersection. A section of his neighbor's fence had fallen.

Rylan crossed the street in a few quick strides and shined his light on the fence, which was still bobbing from whatever had weighted it down. Something dark leaped over another fence and disappeared in a neighbor's yard.

"Hey, I see you!" he shouted to the shape that was no longer there. "I'm calling the cops!"

He reached into his pocket, pulled out his cell phone, and held it up to his ear. "I'm calling them now!"

"You sure you want to do that?"

Rylan jumped to the side. It was Mr. Tandy, the owner of the house with the "Looters will be shot dead" trespassing sign. He was carrying a Remington 870 shotgun.

"Jesus! You scared me to death."

"I said, you sure you want to call the cops? They'll just kick us out if they find us, and if it is a looter, well, we have answers for that here in Texas. Where is your gun?"

"I have a bat."

"Please tell me it's at least aluminum."

Mr. Tandy had an odd-shaped head that seemed wider at the top than at the base, and his eyes were set a little farther apart than most people's, like a cartoon character in a Matt Groening strip. In a way, he could have been Bart Simpson's older, gray-haired uncle.

"What are you doing out here?"

"I heard a noise. Saw you in the street. When you chased after whoever that was, I came out. This is a nice neighborhood, but times are tough. Money doesn't come as easy as it used to, and what money does, doesn't go as far. So I'd keep that bat at your side. And if you can, find a gun."

Rylan thought of the mountain lion, its strong fangs and bloody chin. "Thank you, Mr. Tandy."

"Call me Amos."

Amos held out his hand, and Rylan shook it.

"Rylan Scott."

"You're the one doesn't use his name anymore."

"We changed our last names." Amos nodded with understanding, but gave him the kind of sideways look he gave to antivaxxers, hippies, and liberals.

"Shame people have to meet this way nowadays, Rylan. Used to, before we were all playing on our phones, we had parties in the middle of the streets in the cul-de-sacs, and everybody was invited. Things have changed since then." He nodded to Goliad. "Definitely changed."

Amos walked back to his house, his shotgun crooked in his arm. He waved to Rylan, then went inside.

Between the mountain lion, the person in the dark, and Amos Tandy, Rylan couldn't return to sleep. He went inside and began cutting up more carpet upstairs. He stopped and turned off the light stand when he saw the police car coming down the street. The patrol car cruised and shined its high beam from one side of the street to the other. Rylan waited for it to pass, then got back to cutting up carpet.

He went outside and turned on the generator and plugged in the cell phone to check the news and the weather. Rylan hoped for a cold front. A line of thundershowers was expected in the evening, but the temperatures would stay in the mid-90s with humidity around 75%. Times like this, Houston weather was referred to as a devil's armpit or a cow's asshole, and the metaphor stuck. It was hotter than hell and wet as a cow's ass, too. Not wet from rain, just wet in the air. He couldn't spend more than ten minutes working before his whole body was soaked in sweat. Since Rylan hadn't brought many shirts, he removed his wet one, hung it on the dryer, and wandered his house shirtless.

After the weather came more discussions of repercussions and fallout from Goliad. Its effect on the economy, infrastructure, the oil industry, tourism, and of course, the environment. Nothing that hadn't been said a hundred times before in the past few weeks. There were shots of the interstate so clogged up and full of people waiting to get into Clear Lake that the highway looked like a giant mechanical kaiju fall bleeding arteries of asphalt.

Zone 3 was cancelled for the day and delayed until tomorrow so that people from Zone 2 who were turned around yesterday could get in today. That didn't stop a giant caravan of people from Zone 3 from trying to get in. Some had poster boards and large cardboard signs that read, "WE WANT OUR HOME" and "LET US GO HOME." The cameras were eating that up. One man, a middle-aged man in blue jeans and a navy polo, was being interviewed.

"All I'm saying is that this isn't some third world country run by a dictator. We have rights. This is America, and this is Texas, and these are our homes they won't let us get into. What kind of freedom do you have if you can't go home? You know what I'm saying?"

Rylan understood. So did everyone else hiding in their homes in the Cove. Freedom was a house.

9:00 am

When the air was too suffocating to keep working inside, Rylan went to the backyard and started bringing down the fence with his hammer. It was his dad's old hammer. His backdoor neighbor saw him attacking the fence with a hammer and joined him.

"Hard to believe that a kaiju that wasn't even near my house did all this damage," the neighbor said. "Course, near is a relative term when your body is longer than a 5k. Can you believe that?"

"I take it you're a runner," Rylan said.

29

"It's a lifestyle choice, which means it is a healthy addiction."

"I thought there were no healthy addictions."

"There aren't." His neighbor smiled. "But I did the math. If his fall is five miles long, that means he is at least ten miles to finish a complete lap. With a hundred or two hundred yards from side to side, that means you could conceivably hold a kaiju half-marathon to race around him. Two laps is a full marathon."

Rylan shoved on a split fencepost. "I just want to repair my house."

"I hear you." The neighbor wasn't really moving to help. He just stood there and watched Rylan work. "When he fell, the shockwave was strong enough to rip apart houses within three blocks of the fall. We're lucky we are where we are, or we'd have more than toppled fence posts and broken windows."

"You mind?" Rylan motioned to the fencepost.

"No problem. Glad to help."

They worked on fence posts the rest of the morning. Rylan would push against one side, and his neighbor the other, and then the post would topple like a tiny pine tree. Then each man would grab one end of the fallen section of fence line, and they dragged it out to the front yard where his rolled-up carpet was already waiting.

While sipping lemonade and taking a break between fence lines, his neighbor said, "Saw a damn mountain lion this morning. Can you believe that?"

"I was there. Walked right past me."

"You kidding me? You were outside when that happened? I'd shit my pants."

"Seeing a wild mountain lion covered in blood walking that close to me? A viewing like that comes with some fiber. If I'd been eating better, I probably would have shit my pants right then and there."

"At least the water's working."

"Maybe yours but not mine."

"My bottled water supplier comes around twice a day. Dom Perignon."

"Yeah, mine, too. Brings me a filet mignon every day with it."

His neighbor laughed. "I read that the force of the kaiju fall – by the way, why do we call it a kaiju fall and not a daikaiju fall? It's technically a daikaiju, right?"

"Convention, I guess."

"Largest kaiju to ever make landfall. Of course it lands in Texas."

"Everything's bigger in Texas."

"Including the vermin. But back to my point. This daikaiju is so big, and the force of his fall was so powerful, that it has crushed the water mains in Solemnity Bay. They are trying to reroute water from elsewhere. What a fall. Have you gone to look at it yet?"

"No. Maybe this afternoon. I wanted to get some stuff done around the house."

"I hear that. Be careful. There are all kinds of things out there. People, too. We went yesterday. It's a crazy sight."

His neighbor took a final long drink of his lemonade and said, "I can't believe this happened to us. We've been in the house less than three months. I barely have enough money to pay my bills. We were just getting back on track when this thing happened. Now I'm going to have to pay a deductible? I don't know how I'm going to do it. How long have you been here?"

"A year and a half. I'm hoping the bank cuts me some slack on the house and my credit cards on account of Goliad."

"You work for Tatanka Oil, right? I've seen the logo on some of your shirts."

Rylan nodded.

"So you haven't gotten a check in three weeks, huh?"

"Not since the company went on hiatus and fled Houston. Lucky me, their office building was demolished while Goliad was pushing towards the refineries. At least my wife is still working. What about you?"

"School district. It's shut down, but the checks keep coming. I'm lucky that way, I guess. A lot of people aren't getting checks. That guy living caddy-corner to you, he isn't getting checks no more either. What're you going to do?"

"I don't know. Fix my house. Make sure it is ready for when my family comes home."

"It's our houses. It's all we got, right?"

Rylan finished his lemonade, and then they started back into the fence line. An hour later, both yards were naked and exposed to the outside world. Clusters of thick grass outlined where the fence should be.

"If you get low on food, there are water and food distribution centers. I think the nearest one is in Nassau Bay, but you might want to try League City, too."

Rylan shook hands with his neighbor, then they both went back inside their homes.

Soon after, the garage door went up, and Rylan pulled out in his pickup. He drove to the center of the subdivision so that he could get a good look at Goliad. In East Texas parlance, Goliad was the "sumbitch" that was wrecking his life.

Just like his backdoor neighbor said, the houses within three blocks of the kaiju fall were torn apart. They looked like some Texas god had taken his sledgehammer to the side facing the fall. The siding was crumpled and concave. In some cases, the front of the house was missing, like it had been wiped out by a bomb, leaving behind a dollhouse view of two-story coastal homes.

Then he came to the ridge of pushup from Goliad's fall. The remains of a house jutted out from under the clay like a man struggling to pull himself out of a pit of quicksand. Giant flocks of seagulls and grackles flew overhead. Clouds of flies swarmed above in the hot sun. Large raccoons with full bellies waddled drunkenly over the pushed up earth.

He drove his truck over the rise and down into Goliad's open grave. There were others out there, neighbors he did not know or people who were there illegally. After all the damage that he saw the kaiju take, he was surprised to find that these people were cutting out small chunks of Goliad's skin with nothing more than pocket knives. Hadn't armor-piercing bullets ricocheted off the kaiju's body? He made a mental note to ask Ainsley about the skin.

Other people were photographing themselves in front of the wall of dead kaiju. It seemed strange to Rylan that amidst so much tragedy and loss, people still had time to post photos to the Internet.

He climbed out of the truck and walked up to the son of a bitch that had caused so much devastation and was continuing to cause so much struggle for his community. Beneath him, the lip of Goliad's armor had sunken underground and become part of Mother Earth. Rylan's feet were standing on the cusp where monster met mother. Deeper, man-made grooves had been carved into the creature's thick shell. Something strong and powerful had been used to make the grooves. They were stained red.

Looking straight up, he saw nothing but Goliad towering over him like a mountain of insanity. Looking left and right was like watching a line that disappeared somewhere in the distance. He wondered if this was how the Mongols felt when they first encountered the Great Wall of China. All that forever. All that fate. The Great Wall of Fate, if you believed in that sort of thing. Rylan had heard lots of talk about fate over the past two weeks. Was it fate that the kaiju had landed in Solemnity Bay of all places? Was it fate that Goliad had missed his house? He was an agnostic fate-ist, at best, wanting to believe that there were forces at work here, but the engineer in him believed in different kinds of forces. The engineering mind suggested the attraction of a warm Gulf current or migration caused the kaiju to fall in Solemnity Bay. This was preferred to the idea that pure, blind fate had pulled the kaiju toward a "destiny."

A large woman in a Mumu was kneeling down on the ground and crying. Her hands were placed on the kaiju's corpse. Her husband had his hands on her shoulders as he said, "It's okay, Camille. Let it out."

The stench was strangely not overpowering. If anything, Goliad's corpse smelled like canned sauerkraut.

Goliad's terrible claws were like mountain peaks in the distance. His face remained unseen. He had died facing the bay waters he came from, his horrible face like a lighthouse from hell.

"My father's gone." The large woman in the Mumu, which had a kind of splattered rainbow pattern, was talking to Rylan.

"I'm sorry for your loss," Rylan said.

"It's just his ashes," the husband said.

"It's not just his ashes. It's all I have of him. It's all I have of anything. It's all buried under that damned monster."

"I've stayed through Hurricane 1s and 2s, but this is unlike anything else. Have you ever seen anything as bad as a daikaiju?"

"F5 tornado," Rylan said, not offering an explanation.

She started crying again, her shoulders shaking up and down as her husband guided her back to their Taurus.

Rylan reached out and placed his hand on Goliad. This is what a monster feels like. This is destruction. This is death. It felt cold and hard. Soft on top, but solid underneath, like sand after a rainstorm packed on top of rocks. He removed his hand from the corpse. Then he pulled out his pocket knife. He jabbed it into the skin. It punctured easily, much easier than he had expected. He twisted his knife until he had cut a dollop-sized circle of skin, which he held in his palm and contemplated.

From farther down the Wall of Fate, someone yelled "FEMA!" Cars pulled out recklessly and drove off, bumping and bouncing over the ridge. Rylan waited until the rabbits had fled, then drove down the street and parked his pickup between two others. He slid down in the front seat and watched the FEMA cars drive up.

Rylan had no idea why he didn't drive home. Maybe he just wanted to see the agency in action. If he was being honest with himself, he was spying. He was trying to figure out how they worked so that he could avoid them.

Three cars and one pickup parked, and people in black jackets with "FEMA" in bold, yellow letters across the back got out. One man with a radio was pointing to different sections of the kaiju and saying something to the others. The others took out poles, GPS units, and total stations. Rylan recognized their tools from his college days. They were surveying Goliad. As they surveyed, some spray-painted "X"s on Goliad.

While the others surveyed, two of them, a balding man and a young woman wearing a hijab, put on Hazmat suits. From a container in the back of the pickup they removed a ten foot long pole that looked like a giant metal toothpick, which they slid into the "X"s already marked along Goliad's hide. The spots were measured six feet away from each other and alternated high and low. While the man held the tip of the long pole against Goliad's hide, the woman pushed on the end. The spear point at the end of the pole pierced Goliad's hide as easily as Rylan's pocket knife had pierced it minutes ago. She pressed a green button on the side of the metal beam, and a second beam shot even deeper into Goliad's side. She pressed a red button, and the second beam retracted. Quickly, they pulled the syringe (Rylan could see now that the metal pole was more like a syringe than anything else) and backed away from the skin. A ribbon of blood poured out of the thin hole like a spigot drain and worked its way down the ridgeline and presumably out to the bay.

Twenty minutes after the FEMA agents began working along Goliad's side, Rylan was covered in sweat in the pickup. The agents were getting hot, too. One removed his jacket and put it down on a hedge. Half an hour and a gallon of sweat later, the agents packed up their poles and measuring devices and moved to another block.

The jacket remained on the bush.

Rylan pushed open the door of his truck. His body was greeted with refreshing air. It felt like a cool slap in the face. He then ran to the corner of the dollhouse-looking two-story and checked to see if any other agents were coming. He was answered with the sudden THWIP THWIP THWIP thundering of a military helicopter zooming overhead. It was flying so low to the ground, he could feel the downbeat wind from the blades.

After the helicopter passed and he was sure nobody was coming, Rylan ran out to the hedge. He grabbed the navy blue jacket with the yellow lettering on the back and ran for his pickup. His wheels squealed as he peeled out, u-turning back toward his cul-de-sac.

After drinking an entire gallon of water and emptying the jug, he hung the FEMA jacket on the closet door right outside his foyer and examined it. There was nothing fancy about the jacket. It was lightweight, designed for keeping out water, cold, and any sense of fashion. He smoothed out its sides. Looked at the bold letters and wondered why governments chose such a boring font. He didn't know what font it was, but he was pretty sure it was the font of governments and people without any creative bone. Then he walked upstairs and climbed back into the Secret Room.

The organ/egg was still there. It didn't look any different than it had the day before. No additional veins were anchored into the kids' furniture. (Rylan made a mental note to cut off tentacles that had seeped into the giant Camel-Lot play set that was one of the boys' favorite toys and something he still did not understand at all. Camels as knights? Give him a good ole action figure any day. Then he laughed at the idea of declaring "tentacle cutting" as one of his chores.)

He placed the skin from Goliad on top of the organ. He waited for something big to happen, but it never came. The skin slid onto the floor. He left it there.

From his toolbox he took his measuring tape and went out into his backyard and began measuring his fence line. He wished that the FEMA agents had left a total station along with the jacket.

The posts were six feet apart, except for the final post, which was five feet down. He finished measuring the other two sides of his lawn, which showed that the posts were also six feet apart, and then went inside to eat some potted meat. It was the kind of food his wife shriveled her little nose at, but since he was on his own, he got to eat as much of it as he wanted.

12:31 pm

He climbed up through the hole in his roof and ate his lunch while watching his neighbors. The neighborhood was full of the sound of hammers and saws. Cars were driving into the subdivision again. Rylan guessed that meant FEMA was allowing Zone 2 people back into the area.

Of course, he watched Goliad, who lay across the horizon blocking the sun's orbit. On the other side of the shadowed corpse was the bay, more residential area, and maybe a Wal-Mart if Goliad's death had not decided otherwise. He could never be sure from the videos he had seen. If it was not crushed under the kaiju's back, 146 also lay over there, which was probably how the government was driving in and out of the area. In the sky, large military helicopters shuttled back and forth. Some of them had lines that hung as uselessly as broken legs on a dragonfly.

A cloud of black smoke billowed from the southern end of Goliad. Rylan hadn't seen it earlier because the winds were dragging the smoke south into Dickinson and Texas City.

At the very top of Goliad, he could make out tiny figures that were more FEMA agents and soldiers holding their long needles that they dipped into Goliad like Lilliputian acupuncturists. Unlike the mobile units used lower to the ground, these units were bolted to the dead animal. He recognized the drill collar and Kelly drive modified for kaiju flesh instead of the middle of the ocean. The first rod had a drill head specialized for biological mass. From photos he knew it looked like a leech. This was all the rage back at the office before kaiju came to

Houston. As oil people, it was always interesting to talk about how their tech was being used to quickly decompose kaiju falls.

Now that he was seeing the mobile platforms "in the flesh," he wasn't as impressed. They drilled less than a hundred feet, and they didn't have to deal with fluid blowout. Gas, sure, but blood? The thing was dead. Blood was only going to come out at the bottom, which was why they used the mobile units to hasten that side of decomp.

While he ate, the sun rose in the east over Goliad's carcass. He checked his watch to note Goliad's sunrise. Sharp rays of light silhouetted the roughnecks working the drill. He thought of the scene in Indiana Jones where the Egyptian workers are singing as they dig for the temple of Tanis. In dark humor, Rylan wondered what kind of treasure the agents would find buried inside Goliad. One time he remembered a crew finding a horde of hookworms lurking inside the belly of the beast. If not for the military presence, it could have been a catastrophe that killed hundreds, if not thousands of people. It was also one of the reasons the government hesitated to release people back to their homes until the kaiju was more fully decomposed.

Despite the sun's fight to win the sky, Texas weather had other plans. Thunder rumbled behind Rylan. Dark clouds were amassing, with long smears pouring to the ground. The front was coming fast, too.

"Shit. So much for evening storms."

He gathered up his trash, but dropped an empty can of potted meat, which rolled down the gabled roof and fell over the side of the roof. Rylan jumped down into the hole, tossed his trash, then raced out to the pickup where he kept the tarps. Distantly, he was aware of the change in air temperature and pressure. It was more than that, though. The sounds of DIY construction that had filled the neighborhood were suddenly gone. Everyone was preparing for a storm that would pour into unprotected holes.

Lightning flashed in a sky with a sequestered sun.

He grabbed a royal blue tarp and went to the toolbox. He took his Dad's old hammer and stuffed his pocket with nails, then ran back up to the hole. Water was already dripping on the carpet in John Clayton's room by the time he had all the tools he needed. He crawled up into the rainstorm and cursed his stupidity and misfortune.

He unfolded the tarp shiny side up. He flipped it and hammered a nail through his roof. Placed the ringlet over the nail, then bent the nail back tight with his hammer. He took the other end of the tarp and walked over his gabled roof while lightning silhouetted the neighborhood behind him. A quick glance to the east and Goliad had disappeared behind a sheet of gray. The storm had come like its own kind of kaiju. He hammered the nail with the ringlet already attached, then bent the nail. He found this process much quicker than hammering in a nail, then attaching the ringlet.

The tarp sagged in the hole in his roof. Already a small puddle of water had filled the tarp.

"Fucking fuck!"

Rylan wrenched the nail out, then crawled farther down the roof.

"Should have brought a smaller tarp, Mr. Scott."

He swiveled around, careful to not lose his grip on the wet roof. The tarp was tight now, so he hammered another ringlet into the roof. As he stood up, he slipped on a wet patch of shingle-less rooftop. His foot kicked out behind him, and he fell to his knee. He stood back up and leaned forward, keeping his knees loose. He grabbed a third ringlet and walked as fast as possible into the wind, which was back over the gable. As he went over the top of his roof, he tripped on the ridge vent, the tip of his back boot hitting with just enough force to send him forward into the air. He was two stories up.

Fortunately, he landed face forward and was not wearing his shirt. His skin was much rougher than cotton. Unfortunately, that meant his bare skin was what kept him from falling over the edge and into Buzzfeed for "Dumbest Kaiju Fails." When he stood up, the roof shingles had sand-blasted his torso, which was now covered in a mix of grit and blood.

"God DAMN it!"

Gingerly, he pushed himself away from the edge of the roof. He winced as he nailed the third ringlet in, his blood pooling beneath him and being swept into the gutter. The tarp sagged, but he didn't care at this point. His chest was on fire. He was pretty sure he ripped off a nipple. He scooted on his but back to the open hole and climbed down, pulling the tarp over to close the hole.

The wood was wet, but not completely soaked. He looked down the hole into John Clayton's room and knew he would have to place towels down.

Gently, he made his way over to the ladder.

The egg had changed color. Whereas before it had a blue and black color, it had turned to a glistening whitish pink. He thought of pickled pig's feet, straight from the jar, the way it had that wet sheen to it. It seemed much more alive now than when he brought his neighbors to see it. Even the flat veins seemed charged with life as they stretched full of fluid. He wondered if he cut one of the shoots, would it bleed? They had a definite umbilical cord appearance to them. They were fat and thick. Did they take nutrients from the humidity and pass them into the egg?

He wasn't sure egg was the best word to describe the biomass. Maybe cocoon was better, but cocoon for what?

He placed his hand against the wet wall of tissue. Warmth came from inside, but no heartbeat.

Downstairs, he found a fresh puddle of water underneath the broken front window. He reminded himself to get to it later. With rain pelting his house, he went to the pantry and dug around for medical supplies. Supplies in hand, he went to the bathroom and stared at himself in the mirror. It was worse than he thought. His jeans were ripped from when he fell the first time, and his knee had an inch-long gash. He had cuts all over his torso, across his cheek, and on his left hand from his second fall. On the plus side, he still had nipples! (Why he cared about that, since nipples have no function on a man, he did not know.) Thank God for small miracles, he thought. Little flecks of roof grit had sunk into his cuts. He needed a shower first, but he had no water, and even if he did, there were signs everywhere warning people against using water. Goliad's fall had cut off this side of the Cove's drain system from the rest. There was no place for water or plumbing to drain to.

He walked into the front yard in nothing but his underwear and let the rain wash over him. Thankfully the rainstorm was made of small water drops more akin to a showerhead. He turned into the rain, but that was too painful, so he turned his back on it and let it stream over him. His whitey tighties were stained pink from the blood.

The water was rising too. If the pumps were still working, though, they would be fine. The retention pond and the pumps were on his side of the Cove, away from Goliad's fall. Assuming they still worked.

That's when he heard the dog yowling. At first he assumed it was a dog barking for attention, but there was an edge to it. It was the difference between a baby crying for attention and a pained baby. He wasn't sure if everyone could hear the difference, but he knew it.

He walked down the main street away from his house. He passed his backdoor neighbors. For a second he wondered what he must look like, walking the streets searching for a dog. Oh, well. To hell with it. Whoever was left in the Cove probably had bigger concerns than him. The dog continued to yap, and the sounds were definitely stressed. This wasn't a dog left out in the rain. This was an animal in trouble. And if nobody else was going to respond, fine. He was raised better than that.

A post-apocalyptic pall seemed to have covered Dolphin's Cove. Trash and desolation were the prominent residents here. Most of the houses were still boarded up with protests to Goliad and warnings to looters spray-painted on the boards.

YOU LOOT
WE SHOOT

GOLIAD SPARE US

LOOTERS WILL BE SHOT
TRY US
YOU WONT BE WRONG BUT ONCE

GOD LOVES TEXAS
AND HATES GOLIAD
(A shredded Texas flag was hanging next to the sign.)

TEXAS FOREVER

TRESPASSING IS THE BEST WAY TO MEET THE LORD

He found a two-story house that was completely burned down. The houses to either side were partially damaged. He cut through it, careful not to slip on the ashen boards. The streets were full of flooded water and splintered wood. He pushed aside a wicker chair and walked through the grass. The yelping stopped. Rylan stopped and listened. He thought he had been getting closer, but it was hard to tell. The rain was messing with him. Then he saw the Daos down by the retention pond. They were in their rain jackets and were trying to climb over the chain link fence.

"Hey," Rylan called to them, running up. Jim and Christine looked up at him. Christine looked twice.

"Kaiju take your clothes, too?" Jim asked.

Rylan shot Jim a look that spared no details. "Is that the dog?"

"A shepherd. It's caught on some fishing line down close to the pond, but in this storm, the water level's rising."

Christine said, "If the pumps come on, that dog will drown in minutes."

"Do you have something to cut the fishing line?"

Jim smiled and said something in Vietnamese. By Jim's tone, Rylan realized he had asked a stupid question. Jim was probably saying, "This stupid kid asks a professional fisherman if I have something for cutting fishing lines? Dumbass, I was born on a boat in southeast Asia and was fishing before I learned to walk." Or something to that effect.

Christine said something coaxing back to her husband, probably telling him to cool his head. Jim pulled out a small pair of strong scissors and showed them to Rylan.

"Don't need anything fancy, and I don't want to hurt the dog."

Rylan lifted Jim over the fence, then heaved himself over.

"Be careful," Christine said.

"You calm the dog while I cut the line," Jim said.

Rylan was happy to let Jim take lead on this. He leaned down close to the shepherd, which had begun whining in their presence. He scratched him under the chin, then checked the collar. He recognized the address as a few blocks down. "Voodoo, eh? Hold on, Voodoo. We'll get you out."

The fishing line seemed to be wrapped around the shepherd about twenty times. The dog looked like a fly trapped in a spider's web. The last line trailed off into the pond.

"Probably some kids fishing out here and they got their line stuck on some old log. Then they gave up, cut their losses, and went home. Stupid kids. You don't leave lines out. I'll cut that one last. If I cut it first, Voodoo here will try to run off and only injure himself more. You ready?"

Rylan nodded and began stroking Voodoo's head. "It's going to be okay Voodoo. Don't you worry. We'll cut you out. You'll be running home sooner than you know."

Voodoo wagged his tail.

While Rylan spoke to the distressed dog in soothing tones, Jim worked like the expert line cutter he was.

"In my time, I've cut many things out of line that did not belong there. Turtles, dolphins, human limbs." Rylan didn't want to think what that must be like.

Jim cut to relieve tension. So after one cut was made, another was made so that the section of line could be removed. He worked his way back down the dog, piece by piece.

Voodoo growled low and fought the line.

"Calm down, Voodoo."

The dog kicked out.

"Keep the dog steady," Jim pleaded.

"I'm trying. It's okay, Voodoo. It's okay. Settle down."

But the dog wouldn't have any of it. He growled low enough that Rylan backed off.

"Jim, he's going to bite."

"Almost there."

"Jim!" Christine shrieked. She had seen what Rylan and Jim hadn't. The dog turned about face on Jim, who barely saw the dog out of the corner of his eye. He ducked away in time to miss the dog's snapping jaws. But the dog wasn't going for him. The dog was lunging at something that had been crawling out of the water toward Jim. Something full of teeth.

Everybody screamed as they backed off. The dark-shaped creature struck the dog. Voodoo yelped horribly, then went still as a harpooned fish. The thing dragged the paralyzed shepherd into the rising pond water.

Jim and Rylan leapt the fence in almost a single bound.

Jim shouted in Vietnamese. Christine grabbed on to him.

"What the hell was that?" Rylan said as he tried to see it through the chain link fence. All he could see, though, was rain drops hitting pond water.

"I barely saw it from up here," Christine said. "All I saw was eyes and teeth."

Rylan took a few more steps away from the fence, feeling like a child at a zoo who no longer trusts the fence to keep back the tiger.

"Con Rit," Jim said over the rainfall. "In Vietnam, they are water dragons that attack fishermen. But they are like the Loch Ness Monster. They shouldn't exist."

"Something is existing in our retention pond. Where did it come from?"

Jim shook his head. "Goliad? Wherever it came from, and whatever its purpose, we must call the police."

But Rylan thought of mountain lions in the night and dark shapes that jumped fences. It wouldn't be until later that night that he thought of wild-eyed demons with slavering tongues.

"Maybe we could kill it ourselves," Rylan suggested. "We could lure it out, then get Mr. Tandy and Ainsley and Lisa and shoot it."

Jim shook his head with conviction. "You are an engineer, Rylan. And like an engineer, everything is measurable to you. You think that if you do enough research, double-check your calculations, and bring enough bullets, you can solve your problems. But I grew up on the South China Sea. I have been a fisherman all my life, Rylan. I have seen strange things on boats. Once, I saw out on the Gulf dorsal fins that can only be explained as Orcas. I have no doubt about it. Another time, we dropped our load on deck and found the bones of a person in it, covered in shrimp. I have seen a two-headed hammerhead. And once at night my scanner picked up a shape gliding underneath my boat so large that it made me say Hail Mary's until it disappeared. The point is that some things cannot be measured and reconciled. Sometimes you have to call in for backup, whether that is the police I called for the body or the God I called for the behemoth. This is one of those times you call somebody else."

"But if you call the police, they will take you away. Nobody is supposed to be here past sundown."

"What if next time it isn't a dog but instead somebody's child?" Christine added. "What if we don't hear it next time?"

"I want to protect the kids as much as you. Have two of my own, remember? But instead of making some phone calls to the cops, why don't we get some neighbors and go after it?"

"I won't mention you, Rylan."

4:18 pm

Four hours later, the rain abated. The stop was sudden and proceeded by a cloud break that made lawns steam. The pumps never turned on, to nobody's surprise, so the water remained high enough that some people later kayaked down the streets. The water had flushed the dust and dirt off people's lawns and out into the streets where they lay like a thin oily layer floating on the water.

When the police showed up at the Dao's door in a high-clearance SUV, they didn't talk long. Jim and Christine got in their van and followed the police out of Dolphin's Cove. Their van made a small wave as it pushed through the intersection.

Two other police SUVs remained. From out of one, a woman officer pointed to the house directly across the street from the Daos. A bright blue tarp covered the front roof. The woman and another officer banged on the door. When nobody answered, they threatened to break down the door. They had authority to enter premises to evacuate homeowners for their own safety. That was when the homeowners showed up. The police started yelling, and the homeowners yelled back. The men from the other SUV left their vehicle to provide backup. Ten minutes later, the wife left of her own will in a Jeep, and the husband was escorted, handcuffed, to the SUV. Rifles were confiscated.

Before they left, one of the officers scanned the street and started taking down notes. The other got on his PA system.

"Zone 2 is to be evacuated by sundown. Any residents remaining in the zone will be removed from the area, by force if necessary. We will arrest you. Only three days ago this was a quarantine zone, and it has not been fully cleared for residential return by FEMA. You must leave immediately."

The two SUVs exited the subdivision. Rylan climbed up past the fleshy egg in his Secret Room and took his tarp down. He was much more cautious on the roof this time. He stowed the folded tarp in the Secret Room where it would be easier to get to if it started raining again. That's when he noticed the dollop of Goliad's skin still lying where it had fallen on the floorboards. It had not changed color like the egg. He picked it up and examined it. Something came to him, then. Or rather, it wanted to come to him. He couldn't figure it out quite enough, though, and put the sliver of skin back down on the floor.

Rylan wanted to go outside and make use of the rain-softened earth, but with the police looking for people to bust, he decided to work inside. He had already taken care of John Clayton's room, so he instead cleared out the Secret Rooms. Bins full of Camel-lot toys, little fast food giveaways, a platoon of stuffed animals, and superhero toys were placed in the upstairs den along with a race track and the headboards from an old family bed. Then he went downstairs and cut out the drywall underneath the broken front window where the wall had gone soft. He tossed the drywall out on the pile in front of his house.

The pile in his front yard was growing bigger and bigger. It seemed to be growing by the hour. All those boards and rotted carpet, and now the drywall. It made him nervous. He didn't want the police to force their way into his home because he was leaving tell-tale signs that somebody was living there. Apparently neither did his neighbors because at least some of them were using the pile in front of his house to toss chunks of siding and roofing from their houses. He considered taking the crap and dumping it back where it belonged, but decided against it. He had too much work to get involved in a vendetta. After he verified that only good drywall was left, he made some peanut butter his dinner. Tamara called. She wanted to FaceTime. He put on a shirt and picked up.

"I saw the rain. Are you okay?"

"Yeah. I slipped and cut myself, but I'll survive."

"On television they were warning people not to stay in the zones. They are stilling using chemicals on Goliad, and there are methane leaks, and there are large predators in the area. They don't want people in there. They say Goliad is only thirty percent decomposed."

"He doesn't look any deader than two weeks ago."

"That's what I said, too, but NOAA is saying that he is more decomposed than he looks because of the drilling they are doing. I miss you. You're coming home soon, right?"

"There's still work to do. I want to get a fence up. To do that, I think I'm gonna have to rent an auger and buy some concrete. Do you think you could call around for me? I can pick it up tomorrow."

"What about the police? Won't they see you?"

"They are exaggerating, baby. Everything is fine here."

"I miss you."

"I miss you, too. Hey, I found this." He held up an 8 ½ by 11 photo of their wedding picture.

"We look so guilty." In the photo, which was taken at a winery in Santa Fe, the couple were smiling like they were hiding a secret. The bride wore red, the groom a single-breasted burgundy. Both wore impeccable Star Trek uniforms.

"We were hiding something." Rylan pulled the legal documents out from behind the wedding photo. Each one had a bright lipstick mark in the corner.

"We left those?"

"And you thought I was just being sentimental."

Rylan read: "My name is Tamara May Evans. I ask the Court to change my name to Tamara Evans Scott." He then pulled out the second form and read: "My name is Rylan Edward Brown. I ask the Court to change my name to Rylan Brown Scott."

"I love you, baby."

"I want to get us all back in our house."

"Me, too."

He spoke to his children for a little while until it was time for them to do their homework. They were going to school in Austin temporarily until the quarantine zones were released and the school districts re-opened.

They said soft goodbyes, then hung up. Rylan went to bed and laid down slowly. Most of the cuts had been shallow. Only a few gouges really needed bandaging. Besides gashes on his wrists and one on his cheek that he was pretty sure he incurred thanks to a chain link fence, most of his injuries could be summarized as a layer of skin that the roof had taken from him. Even with the lights of helicopters hovering over the neighborhood and the marbled flashing lights of police cars, sleep came easily to Rylan.

+12 DAYS

2:32 am

He woke up suddenly, the way a parent wakes when their child stands at the foot of their bed after a bad dream, scared to stir their mom and dad, but not wanting to go back to their beds. It was no child at the foot of his bed, though.

He was aware of its presence first and its breath second. Like rainwater, or sewage. Like rotting meat.

The dark shape stretched up from the floor to the ceiling and was standing over his bed, slavering and looking down upon him. He would only become aware of this later as he replayed the image over and over again, like a coach studying game film. It was an image that would stay with him the rest of his life.

The creature had yellow eyes and long, glistening teeth. It screamed at Rylan, flung the door open, and ran across the second story. Its feet thundered across the upstairs floor powerful enough to rattle the photos on the wall. It knocked over some of the Christmas boxes, then dashed up the ladder into the secret place. The roof groaned under the weight of the creature as it leaped up and out of the hole and went…where?

He heard the creature no more. He didn't know if that meant it had run away or if it was waiting for him on the roof.

Rylan remained frozen in his bed, his heart pounding in his throat and his eyes fully dilated to take in what just happened. He grabbed a flashlight and his bat and edged over the bed. Pulled the door open and checked the den. Even though he knew it wasn't there, his mind was pale white with fear and begging him to go back in the bedroom and lock the door. Or better yet, get in the truck and drive away very fast.

At the foot of the ladder to the Secret Room, the hair on the back of his neck stood on end. The tarp flapped against the roof as cool wind blew in through the hole. Thwap, thwap, thwap went the tarp as its plastic slapped the roof. Slowly, he climbed up into the secret place. He hated every groaning step on the ladder that betrayed his location. He shined the flashlight across the room, his bat gripped firmly in the other hand. There was the egg, the hole, and a small carcass. He couldn't tell what it was at first. Then recognition crept into his mind as he recognized the black and tan markings, and he had to catch his breath. It was a pile of fur and bones that used to belong to a dog named Voodoo.

Rylan shined his flashlight up through the hole and waited.

Nothing moved or jumped out. Nothing tried to kill him.

Sweat beading on his forehead, he climbed back down out of the secret place and closed the door to John Clayton's room. Then he backed into a recliner, breathing hard, and dropped the bat. He sat there in the chair inhaling and exhaling and wondering what would have happened if he hadn't woken up so quickly. Black and tan markings. He went through the house locking windows. He even locked the windows with nothing more than jagged slivers of glass left. Downstairs, he checked the front and back door. At the front door he looked across the street to Mr. Tandy's house with the big plywood warning nailed over his windows. The street shined under the radiance of a crescent moon.

He half-expected to see the creature, but the street was empty.

He drank from his gallon jug and sat in a corner chair with his bat and listened and tried to comprehend what had just happened. The long light of the moon through the broken glass sent jagged shadows across the den. Like spider's legs. Rylan felt unsafe in his own home. As long as there was a hole in his roof, he was exposed.

Every scratch of the hedges against his front window, every board expanding or contrasting from the change in temperature and humidity, every sound real or imagined was a sign of the return of the pond monster.

8:14 am

Rylan must have fallen asleep because a knocking at the door jarred him awake. He swung his bat instinctively, then got up. Night, and all its terrors, had gone, but so had the cool air, leaving behind a thick heat almost like fog. Rylan peaked out of the spyhole and saw nobody there. He looked down the block and saw nobody. Did he imagine it? He cracked open the door. A business card fell out of the slit between the front door and the frame. Roofing and fence repair. He went back inside.

Somewhere in the back of his mind, he remembered a dream he had during the soft hours between night and dawn when he thought he was sitting in fear. Dreams just before dawn were always the strongest, like the mind was trying to suck the marrow out of sleep.

He was at the monitoring site for a fracking operation, monitoring hydraulic equipment when the seismometers started going crazy and the whole world felt like it was rumbling.

"Shut down!" he yelled at another engineer for Tatanka Oil. The room was full of engineers and technicians, all of whom were trying to press their respective buttons to shut down the operation.

Rylan raced to the windows. Outside, the hard caliche rose up, then sunk into a giant pit in the ground. A wave of dust stretched out like a ripple in the water. Before the dust could settle, a giant monster rose up. It had thick tusks and small eyes. As the creature turned toward Rylan, he ran out of the monitoring station. He climbed down the makeshift metal staircase to the dusty ground and sprinted away. But he wasn't in the station anymore. He was in the house he grew up in. But it was gone, too, and he was running out of a basement onto the concrete pad. That was all the tornado had left behind.

Behind him, the monster rumbled. Slowly, he turned around. Its shadow stretched from one end of the horizon to the other. The tornado was dark grey at its vortex. The sky behind it was charcoal. Tankers and random pieces of housing and farm equipment were flung out of the tornado, but it did not move. Only stayed there, waiting for him to make the next move.

Rylan ran, and two eyes appeared in the tornado. A shadow formed in the swirling winds. The shape of something monstrous. Claws reached out of the swirling winds.

As he sprinted, the ground underneath him rose up in the palm of the monster's claw. Rylan latched on to a large juniper tree for dear life as the world was lifted thousands of feet into the air. A giant head turned its spoonbill eyes toward him, and he jumped into the void. He was saved by a zip line he hadn't seen before. He was now zipping across the kaiju, his heart pounding. The giant claw reached up to him, and he thought his heart was going to explode in his chest. Then the pounding of his heart became the knocking at his door.

Rylan hated his dreams.

After cranking the generator and making a cup of coffee, his phone dinged. Tamara had texted him. "Order reserved @ Home Srpls n koby. Be carfl. New Kaiju in Gulf."

"Dont worry. I'll be careful. 👍"

Koby was shorthand for Kobayashi, Texas, which was one of the small towns in the Clear Lake area. It had been settled originally by Japanese rice farmers almost a century ago. In some places, it was still possible to find remnants of the Japanese architecture, though most of the original landowners had sold their land to real estate developers after NASA moved into the area.

With little desire to stay inside, Rylan got dressed and emptied out his pickup. He decided it was time to visit the support area in Nassau Bay that his neighbors had talked about. He could use some unprocessed meat in his system. He could also pick up the ordered supplies from Home Surplus and hope that no more kaiju were coming to Houston.

He tucked the FEMA jacket under the passenger-side seat and turned on his police radar detector before leaving. He was pretty sure police weren't searching for high-speed motorists, but any advantage would help. The real problem with getting to Nassau Bay wasn't being spotted by the authorities, though.

The real problem was that Robinson Bayou fed through the area and cut directly into the badly named Clear Lake, which was as clear as mud. (Ironically, Clear Lake was conjoined to Mud Lake. It was all brown water to most residents of the area.) Robinson Bayou cutting through the area meant there were only three roads that could get him from one side of the Clear Lake area to the other: Galveston Road, Egret Bay, and 146. All three roads had barricades operated by state police and Texas State Guard. The government, too, knew how to control the flow of people in and out of the area.

He never got close enough to the barricade for troopers to question him. He circled the area like a disillusioned vulture hoping for roadkill that wasn't there, rechecked his maps, then stopped and pulled over when his scanner indicated police were nearby. But there was simply no other way to get to Kobayashi without driving out to the highway, which had more police and even National Guard.

While driving away from Egret Bay for the third or fourth time, he glimpsed a dirty sedan turning into a Church parking lot, then disappear behind a copse of cypress. On a whim, Rylan followed. He found a dirt road leading out to the bayou, and at the edge of the bayou, he found a ferry. Or rather, a makeshift ferry created by an entrepreneurial man who had plenty of thick plywood and two john boats. He had rigged the motors with a bar so that he could control both of them with one handle. Two hinges and a thicker board made the ramp.

"Do you think you could get me back if I'm loaded down with fence posts and concrete?"

"Been doing it all day, brother."

"What's the cost?"

"Just trying to help people. Whatever you can give me to help with gas, though, I'd appreciate it."

Rylan handed the man a ten dollar bill and shook his hand, then drove the Silverado out onto the ferry next to the sedan. An Indian-American man and his wife, who was wearing a sari, smiled and waved from inside.

Five minutes later, Rylan was across the bayou and driving towards Kobayashi. This part of Clear Lake was much cleaner than the southern side of Robinson Bayou. It was a night-and-day difference. The streets were free of debris and rain water. Traffic traveled as easily as it had before Goliad came ashore. The stores were open and people were walking their dogs.

The parking lot at the Home Surplus Supplies store was full, and he had to wait in line an hour to be helped. When he told the man at the counter about his reserved wood and concrete, the man checked a clipboard, then a hand-scrawled list. He wiped away sweat because there was no air conditioning in the building, then said, "I can't find it. Sorry."

"Are you sure?" Rylan yelled over the roar of the industrial fans that were trying to help reduce the temperature. "My wife called last night. Can you check again? I had to get a ferry to come here."

"Ferry? You come from Bolivar Peninsula?"

"Solemnity Bay."

"You guys got hit pretty bad. I'm sorry to hear that." The man checked the list again. "There is no Rylan Scott listed."

"How about Tamara?"

"Tamara. Nope. No Tamara of any kind. Sorry."

Rylan thought for a second. The man took a deep breath and was about to ask Rylan to move out of line. It had been a very long and hectic week at Home Surplus Supplies. Then Rylan thought of something.

"How about Hiawatha?"

"I don't really have time for this. Do you see that long line behind you? I've been working sixteen hour shifts for two days straight."

"Please, just check once more."

"Hiawatha?"

"Hiawatha."

He looked over the list, started to say no, then his eyes lit up. "Hiawatha. I'll be damned. Your wife should leave it under your name."

It was a joke, a name for a young couple to leave for to-go orders and dinner reservations. Somehow, it grew from there. It was the word they told their kids to trust. If anyone, even a policeman, didn't know the word was Hiawatha, then the policeman wasn't sent by Mommy or Daddy. Of course she would leave it under Hiawatha. It made perfect sense. Whoever set up the order would never forget the name.

Rylan pulled his truck to the back and watched the men load his truck with ten fence posts, thirty three two-by-fours, and four hundred pounds of concrete. The pickup sagged under the weight. Rylan tied down a tarp over the equipment so that nobody could see his cargo, then drove back to Nassau Bay for water and a fresh meal.

National Guard directed him to Space Center Houston, which was the staging area for food, water, and medical supplies. He stood ten minutes in line with fifty other people while a forklift retrieved a new pallet of water. People took entire cases from the top of the pallet. If they could, they grabbed two cases. It was more water than they could drink in a week. When Rylan got to the front of the line, the pallet was empty except for one last case. He picked it up, then turned and saw an elderly woman in a wheelchair. He couldn't leave her out there any longer, even if it meant he had to wait longer.

"Where's your car, ma'am?"

She smiled, put her hands together, and bowed slightly. She pointed to a van with a wheelchair lift. He carried it over and loaded it in the van.

"Do you need more?"

She shook her head and put her hands back together in a sign of thanks.

Rylan went back to wait in line, then after another ten minute wait, got a case that he placed in the back seat of his cab. Then he joined some volunteers who were unloading MREs and handing them out to people. There were enough MREs to feed a city, it seemed. He took his MRE and a hygiene kit that had been handed to him by Red Cross volunteers, then went and ate in his pickup. When he returned to the pile after he ate, a doctor pulled him aside to check his cuts, particularly the cut on his cheek and left wrist.

"I'm okay."

"Did you put anything on this? I don't want to send you downtown because something got infected."

Rylan would not look her in the eyes. "I'm fine. I was fixing my roof and tripped."

"We've seen a lot of that over the past few days. You need to be more careful. More people are hurting themselves trying to fix things they shouldn't be doing. All just to save a dollar. Believe me, it is worth it to just hire the contractor if you have the insurance to cover it."

His heart rate, blood pressure, and temperature was taken. Then his eyes, ears, and throat were checked, too.

"What's your first name?"

"Ryan."

"Last name?"

"Reynolds."

The nurse who was helping the doctor looked up. She was a gray-faced Hispanic woman. "You know, we're here to help."

Rylan shrugged.

The nurse said, "I take it you are from one of the zones that have not been cleared. Calm down. Nobody's going to turn you in. We just want to make sure you're healthy and taking care of yourself."

"You haven't seen anything weird, have you?" the doctor asked.

"Weird like what?"

"Weird."

"No."

The doctor quietly analyzed Rylan's lie for a moment, and right when Rylan was sure the doctor would say something, she handed him some gauze. "Change those bandages every two days, and be careful. We've heard rumors that there are weird things being seen, and not just large predators, although they are in your area, too."

"I'll let you know if I see anything."

As Rylan drove back, he saw two large buildings, one being propped up by the other. A scar, probably from the end of Goliad's tail, scratched across the side of the fallen building. Crews were surveying the fallen building from the top of the other structure.

He passed Egret Bay and went down to Old Galveston Road, then turned back onto the dirt road. He drove slow and was careful to avoid holes where the dirt had washed away. He pulled up to the bank of Robinson Bayou where he had been dropped off.

The ferry was gone. Rylan didn't know if the troopers had seen the man's operation, or if the man had gone home for the day. It seemed less likely in Rylan's head that it was the latter, so rather than wait to be caught, he decided to find another way home.

He had heard much of people struggling to get into quarantine zones from the North. And 146 was for government traffic only. But little was said about trying to enter the area from the South. So he left the area and crossed under I-45. As he had suspected, nobody was guarding the roads leaving town. People here were free to come and go as they pleased. He drove down to Hitchcock and crossed I-45 there, then planned to travel 146 up, but it was blocked. So was Old Galveston.

He had been on the road for over an hour with a heavy load, so he gassed up, then checked out his GPS. Based on blockades, the quarantine zone was everything east of I-45 between Robinson Bayou in the north and Dickinson Bayou in the south. He thought about driving up and down the many little subdivision roads leading up to Dickinson Bayou. Surely somebody was offering ferry rides back into the quarantine zone. Then he decided to try 517.

1:15 pm

Troopers blockaded 517, too.

Unfortunately, Rylan took a bad turn and suddenly found himself in line to enter the quarantine zone, which he knew would not be allowed. Nobody was allowed back into Zone 2. If they busted him, he would be sent back to Austin.

He reached under the passenger-side seat and pulled out the navy FEMA jacket. Could it be that easy? What other option did he have? He put the jacket on and buttoned it up so that his t-shirt wasn't visible. He hoped they didn't ask him to get out of the car. His blue jeans would be a give-away.

As the pickup drew near the inspection point, he wondered what the penalty was for impersonating a government agent. If he was busted, maybe they would go easy on him. Surely, there were other people impersonating FEMA agents. (God, let there be other people impersonating agents.)

The hairs on the back of his head stood on end when a state trooper with a Belgian Malinois approached his pickup. The dog ignored the pickup as the man walked the dog to the next car. He wondered what the dog was sniffing for. Was it a drug dog? Bomb dog? That made no sense. Kaiju dog?

The cars were funneled into a single line, with concrete barricades on either side. He was like a cow in a slaughterhouse with only one way to go.

When it was finally his turn to drive up, the police officer looked Rylan in the eye. Rylan did his best to not blink or look nervous. To act naturally. It was always harder to act natural when you didn't feel natural. Then everything that felt natural felt unnatural and weird.

"Can I see your badge?"

Shit.

"Hang on," he said as he fumbled through his jacket and opened the center console of his truck.

He was saved, at least momentarily, by the Malinois barking at an out-going car.

"Stay there," the officer said.

Only one person, a backup, stayed with Rylan. The others surrounded the outgoing car. The person was asked to exit the vehicle, then asked a few more questions. The man opened the trunk of the car. The officers took a step back, then took the man's keys and drove the car into a church parking lot. When the officer came back, Rylan asked what was in the car.

"Kaiju souvenirs. You know how much a piece of Goliad can get you on EBay? A big-enough piece could put your kid through college."

"Hey, I must have dropped my badge at the hotel. Can I get in, or do you want me to go back and get it? I'd rather not."

"Don't worry about it. Pull over there, and we can make you a new one."

(Almost made it!)

"Thanks," Rylan said, while quietly freaking out inside. The officer had directed him to the Church parking lot. He would have to get out of the pickup truck, which would give him up.

"Know what? I'll just go back and get it. It's not that far away." He started a U-turn in the road.

"You don't have to go all the way back. We have a temporary badge maker. Got it yesterday," the officer said, following him.

"I appreciate that, but I think I dropped it in the parking lot. I want to make sure nobody picks it up."

"Understood," the officer said. "No telling what people here could do with a FEMA badge."

As Rylan drove nervously away from the station, he saw the police officer watching him leave. Suddenly, the man raised his radio to his mouth. Rylan knew it was dawning on the officer that if badges were being stolen, so could FEMA jackets, and a man in a FEMA jacket, buttoned all the way up in this heat was just too much weird. Had his face given it away? Did he look nervous as he turned his truck around? He wished he hadn't mentioned the possibility of the stolen badge.

Whatever the give-away, his truck or his face, he saw a black state trooper's car pull out in the lane and turn toward him. As Rylan entered the feeder road, the trooper's lights turned on and the car accelerated.

Rylan knew the laws of physics were not in his favor. A fully loaded pickup truck would neither outrun nor outlast a patrol car. He had seen enough Youtube videos to know that this would likely end very badly for him. He had to get out of sight and hope that the trooper had better things to do, like helping with the long line of people trying to get back into their homes.

So he did a little urban off-roading. He popped the curve and traveled across a grassy lot as quickly as he believed possible without destroying his shocks. He didn't hear sirens, so once he crossed the lot, he hit the accelerator and turned down a half-road. The cul-de-sac was full of old homes and run-down shops. A few empty cars lined the streets. He went to the end of the cul-de-sac and found a dirt road that wound through cane and underbrush. He had no idea where it went, but now he could hear sirens, and the sirens told him to keep moving. He flew down the winding dirt road as fast as he thought the pickup could handle.

Every washout and bump felt like a car crash waiting to happen. He did his best to avoid the holes, but the road had received little attention over the summer. It was like driving over a scarred face full of acne, and felt about as comfortable. His shocks were being tested, and so was his heart rate. Fence posts slammed in the bed as he hit another hole. A thousand thoughts were going through his mind. Did he just run from the cops? For fence posts and concrete? Could they see the giant wave of dust behind him? If they caught him, would they send him to jail? What was the length of jail time for running from the police? Maybe, he thought, he could pretend he hadn't seen them and was just looking for a way across. The sirens weren't getting any quieter. He hadn't seen a police car yet, but then again, he could barely see anything beyond forest and canes.

He slammed on the brakes. A cloud of dust – his personal contrail – flew flew past him. The dirt road ended in a stand of canes, like a straw wall. He slowly pushed into the canes, and as the first ones fell, he thought against it, parked the truck and got outside. He was glad he had stopped. The canes were blocking his view of a small bayou. Not much more than a four foot drop-off to a pissing stream of a bayou, but it was more than enough to break his axle or at the very least, get his truck stuck.

He backed out and searched for another way out. Thought he saw something. Wouldn't call it a road. It was more like a wide deer path. He doubted he could get through it without at least busting a tire, but the sirens told him not to go back. He put the truck into four-wheel drive.

Slowly, he pushed the truck down the animal path. Small trees no thicker than a quarter bent and snapped under the weight of the truck. Branches scratched and scraped against his rockers. He revved his engine to get the truck to climb over a log. The hood bounced as the front wheel plopped over the far side of the log. The bed bounced when he went over it a second time.

The alligator appeared out of nowhere. It snapped at his tires and scurried off to the side, all five feet of him. Rylan hoped the gator hadn't cut one of his tires.

In front of him lay a low crossing full of mud. Rylan smiled and gunned it. He turned the steering wheel from side to side and let the back end of the truck fish-tail a little. Then the bayou bottomed out in the middle of the mud, and he felt the truck start to stick.

"Shit." He put his weight into the pedal and twisted his steering wheel back and forth. The truck came free like a rabbit escaping a briar patch. The next thing he knew, he was driving down a subdivision road, throwing mud all over the street. He cheered until he came to the pile of skulls.

At second glance, he realized the skulls weren't real. They were Halloween decorations. The guns in the arms of the men and women, however, were real. They got up out of the lawn chairs they were sitting in and approached Rylan's truck. He slowed down.

"I don't want any trouble," Rylan said through his closed window.

"Neither do we, stranger," said an older man with a lean face and eyes like coals. He was wearing an old Astros ball cap, the one with the

Astrodome circled by baseballs flying in a molecular pattern. The man also wore a vest Rylan was sure had extra shells in it. "You live here?"

"Solemnity Bay. I couldn't get through the road blocks. I'm just trying to take care of my house."

Three men and two women armed with shotguns and .22s circled the pickup. Two teens waited by the lawn chairs. They were armed with squirrel guns. One of the men came up around his truck ad lifted the tarp on his bed. He pushed a fence post aside and checked inside. Another waded through the MREs like a scuba diver.

"Hey, those are mine."

"We just want to make sure you aren't trying to sneak anything or anyone inside."

"Sneaking anyone? Who would I be sneaking? I'm just trying to get home, man."

"Do you have an ID?"

"I don't need an ID. This is America."

"Just yesterday we caught some assholes coming through the bayou with vans and pickups. They weren't from around here. They came to rob people's homes. But we made sure no harm came to anyone." The man in the Astros cap pointed back to the way that Rylan came through the bayou. "That there is the only way in or out of the area that isn't covered by a trooper, and we are here to safeguard it. So do you have any ID? I won't ask again."

"Fuck," Rylan said.

"Excuse me?" the old man said, and he raised his Winchester into both his hands. He didn't point the weapon. Just raised it enough to threaten.

"I've got a driver's license. Will that work?"

"As long as it has your address, son, then we'll all be happy and you can go about your business."

Rylan rolled down the window low enough to hand his driver's license to the old man. The old man started to write down Rylan's information.

"Hey, you don't need that."

"Au contraire. We are going to keep this in case we run into any trouble and need to find you, Mr. Rylan Scott of Solemnity Bay, Texas." He whistled to the others, who started to back away from the pickup.

"A word of caution. We're going to be putting up all kinds of nastiness throughout that bayou. You need to find another route unless you want to destroy your tires. Enter and rejoice, neighbor!"

Rylan flipped them the finger as he drove off.

He drove home without incident, parked the truck in the garage, and decided to wait to unload until tomorrow. Lying on his doormat and jammed into his door frame was a stack of flyers and business cards from lawn, gutter, and roofing companies. Rylan gathered them up and threw them on the dining room table. He ate a self-heating parmesan chicken MRE and drank water donated by the Red Cross. Then he went to bed, but not before he locked the door behind him.

Sleep came uneasy to him. If the cold fear of a return of the creature that had visited him the night before wasn't enough to keep him awake, there were sirens, flashing lights, and the occasional gunshot to keep him from finding enough calm to fall asleep. Footfalls on cracking branches and twisting doorknobs, real or imagined, kept him awake until the late hours of the night. When he did finally sleep, he dreamed of dead men dancing like trotting horses on his rooftop.

+13 DAYS

7:22 am

Intense light woke him from fragile, shattered sleep. Rising out of the bed felt like being pried or peeled from the sheets, which were covered in sweat, but whether more from intense, suffocating heat or from fear, he didn't know. He put his bare feet on the warm carpet and walked across the room. He opened the windows to let in fresh air. A hot wind breathed on him, but at least it was new air in the room. He opened the door, half expecting some slithering, foul-faced monster to be standing there in the doorway, its tongue hanging to the side.

The resident of his spastic mind was not there, though. The space was empty. Perhaps it had gotten its jollies the first night, or maybe it was just confounded by doorknobs. Rylan walked downstairs and drank a gallon of water without stopping. Then he walked outside into his backyard and peed on the maple tree until it was covered in a frothy, warm puddle. It was then that he noticed Mrs. Agnew, an older and obese woman who liked to wear leggings and a headscarf like she was riding a convertible in the 50s. Mrs. Agnew was walking her Pomeranian and staring at him crossly.

"Good morning, Mrs. Agnew." He waved. She turned her head up and marched on. The Pomeranian barked at Rylan.

"Ignore him, Benedict." A few quick jerks of the leash ushered little Benedict (eggs or Cumberbatch?) along.

He walked back inside, put on clean underwear, and was about to start his day when a sound hit him so gigantic it rattled the windows (and dropped a few broken panes, which crashed on the uncarpeted cement downstairs). He pulled up the blinds in time to see a small wave of dust and ash blow over the house like a slow phantom hand reaching outward. He knew the ash and dust would be blowing into his house, so he went back to his room and closed the door. He stood by the window and watched and waited for the dirt and ash to settle. While he waited, he called his wife and recounted to her his expedition from the previous day.

"You'll do us no good thrown in jail," she said.

"I don't think they have a jail to throw me into." In the distance, he heard the sirens of emergency responders. By the direction of travel, he assumed they were charging toward whatever made the loud crash.

"Are you sure you should be there?"

"All we have is the house, babe. We can't wait to have another storm do more damage. Or confuse the issue. Can't you just see the insurance company saying that we have to wait while they sort through the types of damage our house has received? I have to get the house fixed, or at least patched up. I took a gamble on driving out of town yesterday. I won't take that risk again. If I don't have the supplies, I won't make the repair. And if I finish early, I will come back to the most beautiful woman on the planet."

"Stop it. Just stay safe."

"I will. There was a loud crash earlier. I wasn't sure what it was, but now I think it was a leg falling. Maybe the ligaments finally gave out on Goliad."

"There's something you're not telling me, Rylan. Something in your voice."

He thought of the slavering monster lurking over his bed, but something inside refused to tell her. If she knew, either she would force him out, or she would come to him. And he had an idea how to get rid of that monster. When the dust settled, he would have the opportunity.

"The engines are running well, Cap'n."

"Aye, aye, Mr. Scott."

He dressed in his oldest, worst clothes and refueled the generator. He primed it and turned it on, then plugged in an extension cord that he carried into the living room. He plugged in the vacuum and picked up the dust that had settled. He had to empty the vacuum three times into the garbage pail. It was already pretty full with MRE packages and processed meat tins, and he knew he would have to add to his debris pile pretty soon, which he didn't want to do because he felt like he was leaving a pretty big clue to his existence in the house. Also, it just felt wrong socially from a health-conscience standpoint. It felt about two hundred years wrong.

He used paper towels and an old duster to pick up the rest, then he finally unloaded the truck. He needed well over an hour to move all the wood and concrete into the garage because he first had to move around his equipment to make room for the supplies. After a short break to rest his back and arms, he lined the bed of the truck with the cut-up tarp from his roof and loaded the bed with several different pruning shears and a five-foot step ladder. He drove out to Kaiju Goliad's fall. As expected, there was no activity on his end of the kaiju. A leg had fallen, a news alert on his phone was telling him, and so all activities were driven to the monster's lower extremities.

The skin was hardening from over-exposure. These creatures came from a deep trench in the Caribbean. They weren't made for sunlight.

The skin felt like thick leather to Rylan. Parts of it were pot-marked from the lashings of underwater creatures, possibly lampreys and leeches or goblin sharks. Other parts were gouged with the thick scars of great battles, possibly with other kaiju down in the depths of the world.

He put on his work gloves and stabbed the beast with a pair of branch shears shaped like a porpoise nose. They were intended for cutting off small, thick branches. Now they were used to spear kaiju skin. He thought of his company's Innovation Award, and played with the idea of submitting this new use of the same equipment as an innovation. Assuming the company didn't go under, of course.

Goliad's epidermis was at least a meter thick, possibly thicker in other parts. Rylan only wanted the upper three inches. He jabbed at the skin with the shears, twisting and turning to get some breakage. He could see why the kaiju were so indestructible. Even working for three inches with a pair of sharpened shears was like cutting through rebar. Rylan had wanted three inches, but eventually gave up and settled for a one-inch deep cut. When he had gained sufficient depth with the smaller pair of shears, he put them away and took out the long-bladed hedge trimmers. In his mind, Rylan drew a large circle in the skin. Then he got to cutting. The skin was light green underneath, and not for the first time he thought of a giant fish.

He stopped every ten minutes to rest and pour water over his head. The heat only made the work that much harder.

When the circle got too tall for him, he backed the pickup next to Goliad and used the bed to give him the height he needed to cut a long circle out of Goliad's skin. It took him the rest of the morning, but by then he had cut a large, ten-foot diameter circle out of Goliad. He was covered in oil and blood. The skin was turning dark green, which he assumed was the proximity of blood to the skin. He didn't think it would break. The skin was like packed concrete. Then again, he knew about pressure, and there could be a lot of pressure pushing against this wall of flesh.

He decided to hurry. He didn't want to be there if a ten-foot diameter hole popped in Goliad.

He loaded the patch of kaiju skin into the pickup. It didn't want to load easily, so he had to maneuver the skin into the truck bed. It was like maneuvering wet Saran Wrap. Concentrating on loading the skin kept him completely unaware of the bulge moving behind him from inside Goliad. Something large pushed and prodded the weaker skin. Reached out for Rylan.

Rylan was oblivious. He leaned down to maneuver the skin, which was caught on the tire well.

Suddenly, a seam in the skin popped. Blood dripped from the seam as Rylan looked down Goliad's length, thinking he heard FEMA agents.

Behind him, rows of circular teeth birthed from Goliad's cavity and reached for Rylan's warmth.

Rylan jumped off the truck. As the teeth lunged for his feet, he closed the door behind him. He heard a thud and checked his back mirror. That's when he saw the giant worm slithering out of the hole in Goliad.

"What the hell?" He reached for his keys and turned the ignition on. The writhing, toothy maw of the parasite slammed against the driver-side window.

"Holy hell!" The engine roared to life, and he slammed on the gas. He had failed to put it in drive, though, and the engine revved in neutral. The parasite's mouth glistened like uncooked fat. There was something dreadful in its pale skin. It was the look of desperation for sustenance. The mouth full of daggers slammed into the glass again. A spider's web of cracks exploded across the window.

Rylan screamed as he pushed the truck into drive and accelerated over the ridge. The truck bounced over the ridge with such force he was sure the shocks were destroyed. He did not check his rearview mirror as he sped home.

He parked in the driveway and climbed out of the truck. He pressed the button for the garage door and impatiently waited for it to close, always expecting a giant worm to come slithering up under the garage door at the last second.

He felt a definite need to wash his hands when he returned inside the house. It didn't make a lot of sense to him. Even if the giant parasite was full of tiny parasites, and even if those parasites would infect him by touch, he never got closer than a window pane to the monster. But there was something so disgusting about the mouthy worm that he felt a need to clean himself.

He opened the door to the garage and dragged the skin upstairs and to the Secret Rooms.

The fleshy egg had gone dark again, but something was different. More long tendrils had grown across the floorboards. They were like creepers searching for sustenance in some alien rainforest. One of them lay like a fallen log over the dog's carcass. Little feeders branched out to the skin, absorbing any nutrients left over. Rylan shivered.

Getting the skin up onto the roof was not too hard since he had already moved all the kids' toys out of the Secret Room. Now it was just a room with a wall slanted like the roof on one side and an opening into James Howlett's Secret Room on the other. The tricky part was maneuvering the thick skin past the egg and up the ladder without losing his balance.

Once on the roof, he took his hammer and some nails and nailed the skin over the hole. He climbed back inside the Secret Room and nailed the underside several times to the top of the roof.

"Try to get through this, fucker." He had driven about fifteen nails through the roof in one way or another. If the slavering monster tried walking around on his roof, it would cut its feet up like Rudolph landing on a roof covered with broken Christmas tree bulbs. Glass ones.

He went downstairs and ate the last of the sandwiches from the Red Cross and downed a bottle of water. Passed out on the couch while he pondered his good fortune. He had witnessed the water-repellant qualities of the kaiju's skin, and he had seen how bright blue tarps were tipping off the authorities that people were living in a house. This skin was as dark as his shingles. While not as revealing and obvious as a bright blue tarp, it would protect his home from the elements.

3:01 pm

The sounds of voices woke him from a thick, syrupy sleep. So thick, in fact, he thought he was dreaming of little dwarfs rummaging around his house, looking for buried treasure.

"Check this one," he thought he heard someone say. The voices came from outside his house, but he was not immediately aware of whether they were in the front or back yard until someone else said "Stand back."

He looked to the front door right as someone knocked. Unlike the police, this sounded more like a gentle rapping at his door. Then the doorbell rang.

Rylan climbed out of his slumber and checked the front door. He saw two Hispanic men in FEMA jackets and slacks. The shorter of the two saw him and motioned to the other man.

"Hey, there's a guy inside."

"Sir," announced the taller man. His head was shaved. "We need to talk to you. You are not in trouble, and we are not trying to relocate people. We aren't cops."

"What do you want?"

"We are going through the neighborhoods and collecting data to determine if your house should be covered by FEMA."

"Maybe we can just talk through the door."

"It would be better if we could talk to you out here."

"No, I think I'm fine."

"I understand your concern, but we need to see ID. People are squatting in other people's homes. If you like, I can call in the police."

"Just a minute." Rylan thought of going for his bat, but it was all the way upstairs. So he grabbed a poker from the fireplace and then opened the door.

The closest one to him was the shorter man. He had a bleached ponytail and carried a clipboard. He had a nervous quality, like he was ready to jump if anyone raised their voice. The other man, the one with the shaved head, had a thick brow and sharp, intense eyes. Rylan didn't trust him.

As Rylan walked onto his front porch with the poker, the FEMA agents backed away.

"We don't want any trouble, sir," the agent with the ponytail said when he saw the poker.

"You never know who you can trust," Rylan said.

"FEMA needs to get some information on your house and determine if your situation qualifies for financial aid assistance to repair your home. But first, we need to make sure you belong in this house. Do you have your driver's license?"

"I do."

"Can we see it?"

"First, show me your ID."

The man with the ponytail and the clipboard smiled. He reached for his wallet and pulled out what looked like a driver's license and held it out for Rylan.

Too late, Rylan realized it was all a ploy to get him to take those last few steps away from his house, for once he took that step to reach for the ID, a bat swung from the side of the bushes and hit him in the stomach. Pain exploded in his gut and Rylan doubled over and fell to the ground. The man with the ponytail planted his left foot on the ground and kicked Rylan in the face like his head was a football and the guy was trying to kick a field goal. The man with the shaved head kicked him in the gut, and a third person (who Rylan never saw) came out from behind the bushes and hit him in the back with the bat.

Before he could catch his breath, the men had stripped the poker from Rylan and taken his wallet. They took all his cash and his cards, then his phone.

One of them grabbed Rylan by the scalp and started dragging him into the house. It felt like his hair was being ripped out by the root. His eyes stung and watered. Then, more chaos erupted. He was aware of people in hockey masks and carrying bats and hockey sticks pummeling FEMA agents. A poker was brandished, and somebody cried out. One of the men yelled something like "Kill those bikes." But that made no sense. You can't kill a bike. You can kill on a bike, but you can't take life from an inanimate object.

By the time he finished pondering killing bikes (which felt like minutes but was probably more like seconds), he realized that his neighbors were his saviors. He was pushing himself away from the melee when the sound of a shotgun blast made everybody stop fighting on his porch.

"The next one sends a hole through at least two of you," Amos Tandy growled.

The men raised their hands and backed away from the porch.

"Call the cops," Amos said.

"You don't want that," said the man with the shaved head. "Sure, they may arrest us, but they'll arrest you, too."

Amos considered this while Ainsley and Lisa dragged Rylan away from his attackers. He couldn't stand upright, and his eye was closing on him.

"Just let us go, and we won't do no harm."

Amos said, "Here's the deal: leave the bat, the wallet, the cash and cards, and the FEMA jackets, and get the hell out of my neighborhood. If you ever come back, I won't fire a warning shot."

The three men took off their jackets. They were wearing nothing but tank tops underneath. Their bodies were covered with prison tattoos – compass stars, cobwebs, and skulls peeking out from behind their tank tops like grim reapers trying to sneak a peek at the world.

The men ran off towards the back of the neighborhood and the retention pond. Rylan hoped that the thieves would try to save time by swimming across the retention pond. Maybe the pond monster would grab them like it did the helpless dog.

"You okay?" Ainsley asked him. He nodded and coughed again.

"It's nothing that won't feel ten times worse tomorrow," Lisa said. She looked at Rylan's eye, which was turning purple. "I'd say put some ice on it, but we don't have any."

"Are you stupid?" Amos said. "Why did you open the door?"

"Yeah," Ainsley added. "We saw the whole thing. We knew you were screwed once you stepped out onto the yard. We tried to stop it sooner, but we had to grab some equipment." Rylan took a good look now that the action was over. Ainsley and Lisa were covered head-to-toe in sports equipment. Shoulder pads, hockey guards, shin guards, football helmets. They were preparing for a beat down. He, clearly, had not.

"I thought they were FEMA."

"They must have stolen the jackets. I've heard they're easier to find than you think. Or they just make them on their own."

"You should all be carrying guns," Amos said.

"We don't believe in guns," Ainsley said, her voice defiant.

Before Amos could begin his soapbox rant, Lisa said, "We are fortunate to have good neighbors like you looking out for us, Amos. Thank you."

"Well, you're welcome. But if you get a chance, you should all make sure you have a gun. Thieving is just the start. What do we do when it's a whole gang, and they're all carrying guns and knives, and they are experienced with them?"

"That's when we call the cops and never mind if they throw us out," Ainsley said.

"I think I'm going to keep the extra bat," Rylan said. It was a short bat, like a kid's, and it had flames up and down its shaft. "Put it next to the front door. That way I have one upstairs and one downstairs."

"You aren't much of a survivor," Amos said to Rylan. At the time, with his head pounding and his eye raging like a ring of fire, Rylan didn't feel like arguing.

"You know they followed you by the tread you left in the ash. Next time, cover your tracks better."

"Leave him alone," Lisa said.

Amos grimaced at the two, then changed topics. "We need to unite. We are better together than we are alone."

Lisa raised her eyebrow.

"Look, I may not agree with your...choices, but I think we can all agree we want to live without harm. And if you think those peckernuts aren't gunning for redemption against all of us, you're bigger fools than I thought."

"So, what are you saying?" Lisa asked. "Do you think we should start going on watch or shooting at anybody who we don't think belongs in the neighborhood?"

"I'm not a gun nut."

"Nobody is. They're just defending their right to bear arms, even at the cost of other people's lives."

"If anybody's a nut, it's you two fruit loops!"

"Fruit Loops? Do you even know what you're saying? Fruit Loops aren't nuts!" Ainsley and Lisa were standing toe-to-toe with Amos.

Rylan raised his hand.

"That's the problem with society today. No respect for the past," Amos said.

"The past? How about no respect for civil rights, you backwoods reject?"

Rylan slammed his bat against his brick wall. The tight pitch of aluminum against brick got their attention.

"Amos, what is your plan?"

Amos looked from Rylan to Lisa and Ainsley. "We all have fences that need to be repaired. Hell, y'all and I share a fence. I merely suggest we join forces for a while. Help each other put our houses back together."

"I like it," Rylan said. "Kind of a superteam mash-up."

"Safety in numbers."

Rylan looked to Lisa and Ainsley. Lisa shrugged. "I don't' know. Have you seen Goliad? His ribs punctured his skin this morning. I swear you can see those giant rib bones leaning our way. Rebuilding could be pointless."

Ainsley took Lisa's hand. "We have to hope." Lisa sighed and nodded to Amos and Rylan.

"We can begin today if anyone wants," Amos added.

"I think I need to lie down," Rylan said.

"Yeah. And we need to make arrangements to get supplies," Lisa said. "Ainsley has some family in construction. They are helping the Government build temporary structures near the tail of Goliad. They were going to use the opportunity to bring us supplies."

Rylan groaned. Lisa thought it was for the black eye. "You poor thing," she said. Her eyebrows furrowed as she followed his line of sight, though.

"Aw, hell," Rylan growled as he stood up from leaning against his house. The giant worm from earlier in the day had made its way up the street. It was writhing on the road. Its skin was gunky and blackened from the heat. As a parasite designed for living inside giant kaiju, it was not meant for the outside world. Thick rolls of worm flesh pulled back as giant teeth protruded from its mouth. It sensed their heat and turned toward them, like a blind killer searching with his hands spread out, hoping to grab onto something he can strangle.

Amos walked to one side and looked to Lisa and Ainsley, who stepped away from Rylan and waved their arms and shouted at the monster.

The mouth hardened as it desperately searched for body fluid. The thought made Rylan shudder.

Amos fired his shotgun on the worm, and a chunk of its head vanished in a red cloud. Intestinal parasites don't scream, but they do turn pale and try to escape. The parasite, frantic, fled to the nearest, coolest place and tried to escape down the gutter. It shoved its giant head into the gutter opening. It was way too thick to fit through the opening, though. It turned on Amos, who had already pumped the shotgun. With a new shell in the barrel and the worm coming at him, Amos fired again. The worm snapped back and fell down on the ground. For good measure, Amos shot the monster a third time.

"We're going to have to clean this up," Amos said.

"What's this we stuff, Kemosabe? I don't remember signing on for worm scraper duty." The two wives left Amos and Rylan to deal with the worm.

"Tomorrow morning. Early," Ainsley said.

"They are a piece of work, aren't they?" Amos said as Rylan helped him drag the worm out into the middle of the intersection. It was heavy and sticky, like tarmac in August. Amos had decided the best thing to do was burn it up, but they didn't want to risk a grass fire or tip off anyone to their location.

"They pay their taxes and don't hurt anyone, which is a lot more than I can say for some people I've read about in the Chronicle."

"Texas just isn't Texas anymore."

"No, it's a whole lot different now," Rylan said as he stared at the dead worm. He grabbed a bandana from his garage and helped Amos gather kindling, which was not hard to find. They just scavenged the detritus that lined the intersection like timber washed ashore on an apocalyptic coastline. They stuffed fence boards and cardboard under the monster's body and shoved used dryer sheets and lint into the worm's orifice where its mouth used to be. Then Amos pulled out a fire starter and lit the kindling.

The fire took a minute to catch. While they waited, Rylan pulled his bandana over his mouth. The monster stunk like an open grave of a fresh corpse with its belly popped open. He spit about twenty times while Amos brought out a bottle of fire fuel, which he poured on the worm. The worm caught fire and started snaking around in the flames.

"Aw, that's gross," Rylan said, and he doubled over. His gut still hurt like he was trying to shit a rock, but now this smell was making his stomach do somersaults. He needed to sit down for a minute. When long, thin worms started pouring from the parasite's wound like sausage from a meat grinder, Rylan lost every good thing he'd eaten in the past twelve hours. The baby worms could not escape the fire. Amos walked over, waiting to stomp on anything that got free of their fiery birth.

"Come here. Let's get some fresh air." Amos led Rylan inside his house. His furnishings were antiquated. Leather sofas with brass rivets, wood paneling walls, and a few deer trophies mounted to the walls.

"Is that what I think it is?" Rylan asked as he crossed the room. The black cube sat on an old microwave cart.

"A Zenith. I give the Japanese credit for this: they make damn fine television sets."

Rylan ran his hand over the wide top of the television set. His parents moved to flatscreens when he was in middle school.

"I bought a converter from the store and have been fine ever since. Nobody's going to force me to buy a thousand god-damn-dollar television set."

Amos went to the hallway and flicked on the light. "I got something even more impressive back here." When Rylan didn't move, Amos said, "C'mon. I won't bite."

Rylan followed him down a hallway with several photos of Amos' family. They all felt old and stale. Again, like Amos had fought hard to join the digital age. Rylan had at least three digital photo frames. Upstairs was an old flatscreen he had rigged into a digital photo display.

The room had a large white flag, similar to the one hanging outside Dolphin's Cove, except where that one had a kaiju, this one had what looked like an M16. Next to this flag was an old Texas star flag from the revolution. A replica, certainly, but well kept. Surrounding the flags were guns of all types of description. Old blackpowders and Winchesters, modern Remingtons and Smith & Wessons. Rifles, pistols, and multi-shots.

"I am not a gun nut. I am an enthusiast, however."

"Is that a Colt?"

"That's an actual Colt. The real thing. Not a display."

The engineer in Rylan felt like a kid in Disney World. There were so many different kinds of guns. They were practically different species, and they all worked differently and the same, with one purpose.

"Amos, why do you have all these guns here?"

"First, I don't show my collection to just anybody. So this is between me and you."

"Okay."

"Second, I believe it is our civic duty to be prepared to handle any threat, whether it is gangs, kaijus, or even our own government. Now, don't look at me that way. I'm proud to be an American and I take off my hat for the National Anthem, but all systems, substantially big enough, become corrupt. That includes ours. I've heard all the arguments about gun violence and how effective they would be in a gun fight with the US Government. But I believe that above all else, one must be prepared to defend this land against all threats. I wanted to show you this for a reason. I wanted you to know it was here in case anything happened. To me, to the Daos, to our other neighbors. They don't see things the way you or I do, but they may need our help regardless. You could carry on the fight."

Rylan wasn't sure he saw things the way Amos did, either. He was in the minority in his way of thinking, though, it seemed.

Amos opened the drawer to a cabinet that, like the wall, was full of weapons.

"I want you to keep this with you until this second kaiju is gone and everything has gone back to a generally normal state." He held out a Glock. Rylan didn't hesitate. There was a monster crawling through his attic.

As they walked out of Amos' house, Ainsley was walking towards them across the grass.

"Guys," Ainsley said. "You need to come look at this."

Rylan had been inside their house before, but this was Amos' first visit. He was admonished by Lisa for not wiping his feet outside, and the shotgun had to be left in the foyer with Rylan's Glock. Everybody then took off their shoes. Rylan remembered this from the last time he was in their house. Even if the house had been ripped into a hundred pieces with no discernable roof, he was pretty sure Lisa would have insisted they take off their shoes. Some people just had a higher sense of cleanliness than his, Rylan reasoned.

The inside of Lisa and Ainsley's home looked like a demo house. It was very chic without being too specific. There were pictures of ships and sunsets on the walls and little bowls full of potpourri on the coffee table, which looked straight out of Crate and Barrel or Pier One. The walls were all painted with neutral, modern colors. The floors were tiled and the counter was granite. The house was so clean that it seemed that even motes of dust dared not appear floating in the sunlight for fear of a vacuum.

"Your house is…" Amos could not finish.

"Not what you expected?" Lisa asked.

"I don't know what I expected. Maybe a lot more, well…"

"Dust?"

"Your abode is impeccable. I'm sorry for bringing in dirt."

"Don't worry. She'll clean it later," Ainsley said from the den. "Get over here and take a look at this."

Rylan walked into the den. Because they owned a whole house generator, the television and air conditioning was working like the power had never gone out. Rylan wished he'd thought to buy one. The television volume was muted. Captured in beautiful high definition on a large-screen TV was Goliad's long form drawn over Clear Lake and Solemnity Bay, Texas. His skin had split down the middle, exposing black and green organs that distended outward. His giant ribs, the size of skyscrapers, seemed to be floating in his own meat as a chopper circled above. Clearly, one of his legs had finally separated at the ligament. In other places, crews were working desperately to sever the legs quickly while doing as little damage as possible. Lower, down near the lake, Goliad's tailbones dragged into muddy waters. Here, the camera zoomed in on the tailbones. All kinds of sharks and gators were attacking the meat, while scavenger birds snuck meals as opportunities arose. In some parts, there was nothing left besides bone.

"That's not what I wanted you to see," Ainsley said. She fast forwarded through the news report that she had recorded on her DVR.

When she stopped fast forwarding, she also unmuted the volume. A tanned reporter said, "I want to caution you. What you are about to see might disturb you."

The screen showed a Doppler that covered the lower Caribbean. The same small kaiju that Tamara had warned Rylan about seemed to be floating across the bottom of the screen towards Mexico or Texas. But on the other side of the Gulf, north of the Caribbean, a swarm of tiny red forms like ants were spreading out from the Puerto Rico trench.

"Dear Lord in Heaven," Amos said.

"People in south Florida and Miami are being encouraged to evacuate," the reporter said. "Residents of the Keys are under mandatory evacuation until five am Eastern Standard Time. After that, they will be encouraged to shelter in place until the swarm passes over. I have with me Dr. Ketchum, the Director of Kaiju Services for NOAA appointed by President Carver. Dr. Ketchum, is it appropriate to refer to this as a kaiju swarm?"

The screen split, and a leathery man with mahogany skin and light-colored hair who had the vibe of an academic who spent most of his time working outdoors instead of researching in libraries said, "We've never seen anything like this before, Maria, so I don't know that we can give it an official title yet, but the way the kaiju are fanning out across the Atlantic, I would refer to it as a swarm. Following the kaiju nomenclature, this would be swarm Grass Fight, as Goliad came less than three weeks ago and Gonzales appeared yesterday."

"That's bullshit," Ainsley said. "Swarms are for insects. There is no classification for kaiju. You're better off calling them a herd, or better yet, a school."

Lisa put her hands on Ainsley's shoulders. "You know it's just media hype," she said.

"Let's cut to the chase, Dr. Ketchum. How deadly will this swarm be? It seems to have the potential to be the deadliest attack in US history.

This could be worse than Kaiju Pearl. This could be an onslaught of Florida."

"There are many factors to consider before we make any determination, Maria. For one, we don't know where and how many will make landfall. Half those kaiju could end up dying in the Everglades, and they won't harm anyone."

"I apologize, but I must cut you off, Dr. Ketchum. We have just received breaking news footage of Kaiju Swarm Grass Fight. Again, I am being asked to warn people that these images could be disturbing."

Lisa hit the mute button. "I hope you don't mind, but I'm getting real tired of listening to her."

The camera was perched atop the cruise ship and angled forward. People were sunbathing and kids were splashing each other in the swimming pool. Families were squeezing the last remnants of summer out of a late Caribbean cruise. From the port side of the cruise, large waves appeared, like masses of boulders moving under the water. Immediately the ship's horn blew the alarm and people jumped out of their chairs. Parents waved at their children to get out of the effing pool now while others ran to the port side to watch the swarm of kaiju. The camera turned slightly on an electronic gimbal to scan the bright blue Caribbean waters.

Dozens of kaiju forms swam at the water's edge. They were like shadows of mountains passing underneath the ship, which veered starboard and then back to aft several times. Then one of the kaiju knocked against the hull, and a second alarm sounded. The screen went back to the reporter. Ainsley turned off the television.

"So, did everyone else see the red dot still heading in this general direction?" Ainsley asked.

"They won't divert forces here to protect us," Amos said. "South Florida is about to turn into World War Kaiju."

"Now, let's all not start making rash judgments. We don't know anything except that…."

Rylan's cell phone buzzed. It was Tamara.

"I've gotta take this."

He walked into Ainsley and Lisa's kitchen. Copper pots hung from a baker's rack. Italian tile was the backsplash over the sink and oven.

"Hey, honey, how are you and the kids? Is everything okay?"

"Have you seen the television?"

"I just saw the Doppler."

"Then you know that everything is not okay. Rylan, that kaiju is getting closer to you."

"It's one kaiju, and it's still got a lot of different directions it can go."

"But all the forecasts look like a second hit on Houston."

"Okay. You and I both knew that this sort of thing happens sometimes and that this was a possibility. Scavenger kaiju have been known to follow dying kaiju before. They also don't tend to rampage across the coastline."

"That doesn't help when you are standing less than a hundred yards from the kaiju that's going to be scavenged."

"It's farther than that," Rylan said matter-of-factly, missing his wife's intent.

"You know there's that part in the horror movie where black folks are like 'why is that white girl staying in the house? She should just run the hell out of there.' Honey, I'm telling you: you're Jamie Lee Curtis."

"You know, she survived those movies."

"Rylan, I don't want you there. I don't feel comfortable."

"I understand. But I've come a long way. I've made a lot of repairs, and we actually stopped a couple of guys who were trying to steal from the neighborhood. So I don't want to run when we don't know for sure."

"But what if…"

"If the worst thing happens, I can be in Austin in four hours."

"Please tell me this doesn't have anything to do with a kid and a tornado."

Rylan went stone-like for a second, then said, "Baby, this is our house. You know what that means."

"It can be rebuilt."

"When the insurance companies and the Feds decide to stop arguing about who foots the bill. You know when Bloody Ridge hit Galveston, it took years for some people to rebuild."

The phone went silent. Then, "Okay. I feel like an idiot."

"A beautiful idiot."

She laughed. He could tell she was crying. Her nose was stuffed.

"We need to talk about a cut-off. At a certain point, to hell with the house. It's too dangerous to stay there, and I just want my husband back."

They hung up the phone and Rylan went back into the living room.

"We're staying," Lisa announced.

"Good. We've got work to do."

They made arrangements to get together early the next morning, at 6. Everyone decided it was too hot to work outside between 10 and 4. They would also take three-hour shifts at night to watch over the block. This was Amos' idea. Rylan was given the early morning watch so that he could get some sleep. Amos would take the first watch, and Lisa and Ainsley, both night owls, volunteered for the middle watch.

Before they left, Amos started to unbutton his shirt, saying to Ainsley and Lisa, "Here, I want you each to have one."

Rylan looked to Ainsley and Lisa who had glanced to each other. All were wondering what the hell the man was going to offer. He had always been the weird one on the block. Part of it was just his way of looking at you but looking somewhere else. Part of it was the theories he had, which were always a little delusional. He had a theory for why avocado trees didn't grow well there when citrus trees did. It involved some kind of fly and the battle for jobs between California and Texas. So when he said he wanted to show them something and started unbuttoning his shirt, it could have been anything.

"Sorry I didn't tell you about these," Amos said. He pulled out two Glocks.

"You were carrying in my house?" Lisa said.

"It is perfectly legal, and I have a license. More importantly, I want you each to take one, temporarily, until this kaiju business is settled. I don't want another worm or mountain lion incident."

They had to stop then so that Rylan could tell Ainsley and Lisa all about his encounter with a mountain lion. When he was finished, Amos, who had been waiting patiently, handed Lisa and Ainsley a Glock 17.

"That is loaded," he said. He showed them the safety and how to load and unload the weapon. "I don't have to tell you to only point it at something you intend to kill."

Lisa handed hers back. "We're good."

"You think you can fend off giant worms and mountain lions with hockey sticks?"

"That's not an issue to us, Amos. No guns in our house. We are breaking a major part of our belief system by not kicking you out." Ainsley handed hers back, too.

"You people are weird, you know that?"

"We're the weird ones?"

"Seriously, are you commies?"

"I think it's time we leave," Rylan suggested as he gently maneuvered Amos to the front door. Amos, for his part, stopped talking. He put on his loafers, took the shotgun, and walked outside.

Ainsley held Rylan back in the foyer.

"Do you think the kaiju and the egg are connected?"

He shook his head. "As far as I know, nothing like that's ever happened before."

"Well, think about it. You are protecting your house from being ransacked by people, but what kind of damage do you think's going to happen to your house if that egg opens?"

He nodded and left.

Outside in the late afternoon, the neighborhood was full of the sound of hammers, saws, and drills. Down the street, he saw one of the Dao's neighbors who avoided being picked up by the police. He was carrying a sheet of plywood to his backyard. On top of another house he saw two men pulling a plug of kaiju skin tight over a hole. He guessed he wasn't the only one with that idea.

Large flocks of birds flew overhead. They weren't leaving until the food source was gone. He assumed that might change in a few days if Gonzales came ashore. He also took note to learn more about the Battle of Gonzales and Grass Fight. He couldn't remember them. It had been a long time since he had taken Texas history.

"It's good to have neighbors you can count on," Amos said. He had to agree. He felt safe among the sounds of work. It was the sound of civilization, and it was more comforting than cell phones and honking horns. It made him feel part of the world again. He hadn't realized how segregated he had felt the last few days. Like a man on a small Pacific island.

He shook Amos' hand and walked back to his house. He placed the Glock on the front table and went upstairs to his bedroom. He looked at himself in the mirror. His shirt was covered in worm gore, and his face looked like he had tried to go two rounds with George St. Pierre. It was tender to the touch, and he had nothing to reduce the swelling, so it was only getting thicker and thicker. He took some ibuprofen from the medicine cabinet and popped them, then took off his shirt and groaned. He had been feeling like somebody'd kicked him in the nuts ever since he took a bat to the stomach. Now he had the proof. He could see the outline of the bat in his gut, and he was glad that there was no internal bleeding.

3:41 pm

He was about to lie down to let the anti-inflammatory do its work when he heard a gunshot. It was a loud blast, like Amos' Remington 870, and it sounded like it was coming from the front, so Rylan went to check on Amos.

The problem was not Amos' house. It was in the driveway of the house catty-corner to his. He had to cross the intersection and the long burned worm that was nothing more than a smoking stain in the asphalt. Still, he didn't want to step near it.

The body sitting in the folding chair in the driveway leaned to one side. Half his head was gone. The shotgun lay on the ground. A photo lay in his lap. It was a younger him with a beautiful wife by his side. The picture was taken on a tropical beach with a crystal blue ocean behind them. She was in a white bikini and wrap-around, and he was in swim trunks. The body in the chair was much older than the one in the picture, but had the same build.

Neighbors were slowly coming out of their houses. It reminded him of the march of the dinosaurs from Fantasia, though he did not know why that image came to his mind. Maybe it was because everyone was stopping their rebuilding, an exercise which could be as pointless as the dinosaurs' attempts to survive. For the dinosaurs, there was an extinction level event in the form of an asteroid. For the Cove, it was Kaiju Gonzales.

An older mother was already there. She stood in front of the body crying. She turned to Rylan. "He lost everything," she said.

Rylan first emptied the man's shotgun.

"That could be evidence," the mother said.

He nodded, then put the empty gun back down beside the man and wiped the stock and trigger with his shirt. Then the old woman handed him the letter. It was brief.

"Cancer took my wife.

Government took my job.

Goliad took my home.

Sorry to everyone that this will hurt."

"Shit," Rylan said. Neighbors circled the man, handing around the note. Few knew him, yet they all mourned him. Lisa, Ainsley, and Amos appeared as faces in the crowd. Someone brought a tarp, which Rylan helped place over the body. Another woman said an Our Father. People held hands while she recited the prayer. Some joined her.

Then somebody said, "I called the police. They are on their way."

That's when everybody shuffled off back inside their homes and waited for the police, who waited for an ambulance. Unlike the other times the police appeared in the Cove, there were no big announcements this time. The police didn't go door-to-door, though they did escort out the people who called in the suicide.

Rylan slumped in the sofa, looking at pictures of his wife and children. He didn't know what the future was going to bring. He didn't know if he would have the strength to carry on where that man had lost his will to live. He would rebuild his house a hundred times over, though, if that's what it took to keep his family alive.

12:21 am

Weight groaning against the floorboards upstairs woke him. Despite his face feeling like it was on fire, he pushed himself off of the couch and stared at the ceiling. He waited, hoping that it was just wood contracting at night. But then another floorboard creaked. The sound had moved from John Clayton's room to the kid's hallway. Rylan's stomach turned icy cold. The Glock was in the foyer practically on the other side of the house.

He crawled out of the couch and stayed low to the ground, walking around the coffee table to the far couch. He heard more footsteps and stopped. The creature went into his bedroom. He knew he would only have seconds once the creature realized he wasn't in his bed. He ran as quickly as he could to the foyer. He could see the Glock, like a black L in the iron dish with his change and keys. The baseball bat with the painted flames was resting against the frame of the front door. His hand was just a few feet from the gun when he saw the creature out of the corner of his eye. He pulled his hand back and retreated to the opposite side of the foyer wall.

The creature's footfalls changed as it descended the stairs. It started on all fours at the top of the stairs, but by the time it reached the bottom, it was back to walking on its hind legs. Rylan resisted the urge to open the front door and run out into the yard screaming for help. He didn't know what time it was, but odds were that it was Ainsley or Lisa that was awake. Even if they saw the monster chasing him out into his yard like the villain in a slasher flick, what could they do? They had bats and hockey sticks, and as much as he respected their decision to not keep firearms in the house, what good would a hockey stick do against the slavering monster?

I don't' want to die, he thought.

He could hear the creature breathing on the other side of the wall. It made a sick, sucking sound when it breathed, like it was struggling to inhale. He imagined it there. It was standing within feet of him, its mouth full of serrated teeth and drool. Its tongue gliding back and forth in the air like a snake with a mind of its own. Its eyes wild and intense. The image of that creature in his mind made him shudder. Cold sweat dappled his forehead.

The creature put its claw on the wall. Its fingers were more boney manipulators than fleshy digits. The way those digits wrapped around the wall reminded him of bug videos where they show close-ups of the bugs eating and grooming themselves. In those videos from his memory, feet were more like branches than fingers. And this is what he thought of as the hand/foot held the wall above him: it was like a branch. But it also meant that the creature was moving away from the foyer and into the living room. He could enter through the dining room.

This is my house, and I don't want to die in it, he thought. Not tonight.

At the last minute he changed his mind, and went back around and directly into the foyer the way the creature came. The creature was not there at all. It had changed course, too, and walked through the dining room. If he had continued…

He could not hear it downstairs. They were on the bottom floor. Only tile and concrete here.

Rylan reached for the gun and felt better with its weight in his hand. It was not a heavy gun, but it felt good to be gripping it in his fingers. He felt confident right up until the creature charged him, screaming.

He shot the Glock twice. White hot fire lit up the night. The sounds came later, and by then, the monster had knocked him into the corner of the foyer and began its retreat upstairs. Rylan fired blindly two more times. The creature jerked forward, and he knew at least one bullet had found meat. He pulled himself up and ran after the creature, shouting "Get out of my house!"

Adrenaline surging through him brought him to the top of the stairs much quicker than he thought possible. He got there just in time to see the creature jerk down the kid's hallway. The thought of the creature walking through his son's bedroom sent a new wave of fear down his spine. But there was something else there, too. Anger. That was his son's room, damnit.

Rylan crossed the den and bolted up the ladder to the Secret Room, not thinking of his safety or the tactical disadvantage he was giving up. He just wanted the damn thing out of his house for good.

"Get the fuck out of my house!" he yelled as he entered the Secret Room.

He placed his hands on either side of the opening and pulled himself onto the landing. The creature screamed from deeper in the room. It was standing beside the egg, its long slavering tongue rubbing the egg like a good luck charm. Rylan fired again, this time hitting the foul creature in the head. The creature fell backward. He shot it three more times until it stopped moving. Then he aimed his gun at the egg and fired five times on it. The egg turned red as he fired his weapon. Rylan slumped against the wall and slid to the ground. He waited to see if the monster moved.

The monster did not move, but the egg had not died either. By the time Ainsley and Lisa and Amos had gotten to him, the egg had actually pushed the bullets outside of its fleshy shell. He heard the lead plinking against the floorboards.

"What happened?" Lisa asked.

"Are you okay?" Ainsley added.

"I killed that son of a bitch," Rylan said, pointing with his gun. "This is my house."

Lisa went around the egg and prodded the creature. It did not move. "I think it's dead."

Amos looked around the room in that weird way he had of looking without directing his attention on any one thing with his side-set eyes.

"What happened, Rylan?"

Rylan told them everything from falling asleep to chasing the demon up into the Secret Room. "I kept thinking of that guy and his note, about losing his house to Goliad, and I wasn't going to let the same thing happen to me. Nobody's taking my house. Not the government and not some damn monster. This is my house."

"Hell, yes, son. Now you're thinking straight," Amos said.

They helped him place the monster on the tarp he had used to cover the hole before he started using Goliad's skin. They dragged its body outside and left it lying next to the oak tree because they had no other place for it, and there was no way in hell he was going to let this creature, which had been torturing his nights ever since he came back, stay inside his house.

+14 DAYS

Rylan slept in. Amos volunteered to take his watch, too. Rylan didn't wake up until after noon, and then it was too hot to work on the fences. But Lisa and Ainsley had gotten word out for the supplies, and they were even getting an auger, which would be delivered sometime the next day. Rylan called home, and his wife and kids were doing well. Tamara was much better. Her code was going well today. Kaiju Gonzales had not strayed its course, though. It was still heading to Houston. They decided that three days from then, Rylan was returning to Austin, home fixed or not.

Rylan still did not tell his wife about the monster or the egg in the Secret Room.

+15 DAYS

12:05 pm

The ribs jutted from Goliad's corpse like a set of white scimitars. The scimitars no longer appeared to be leaning toward them, they were definitely leaning toward their side of the subdivision. A few local news agencies had picked up on it and were reporting predictions on where the ribs would fall and what kind of damage would be done.

The sound of choppers, troopers, and agents had died down since Goliad's belly ripped open. FEMA agents were spraying chemical compounds on Goliad to help devour his insides, but mostly it was the carrion eaters that did the heavy lifting. Rylan had never seen so many turkey buzzards in his life, and they were all disgustingly fat and bloated.

The swelling in Rylan's eye had gone down, but it was still crowned with thick purple. He looked like he was wearing makeup.

At mid-day, his kitchen clock shined 12:00 in bright digital letters. Rylan didn't notice for five minutes because he was working on a drain. When he saw the flashing light, at first he didn't think anything of it. He drank some water and prepared to go back under the kitchen sink, but it slowly dawned on him what the flashing light signified.

"Sweet," he said gleefully.

He ran to the thermostat and changed it to cool and waited. Half a minute later, the AC kicked on. It was the most beautiful fucking sound he'd ever heard. He closed the blinds and the doors and sat directly under the cooling vent until he was chilled to the bone. It took until nightfall for the house to cool down, and then he slept soundly.

+16 DAYS

6:12 am

The ribs leaned toward the houses at a 75-degree angle, like teeth turning ever toward a meal. The skin and fat had peeled back, like a diseased gum line, exposing painful teeth to the elements.

Rylan was concerned, but somehow these immutable problems seemed a little less prescient with a fresh mug of Columbian made from the coffee maker, not brewed over a portable stove. With the air temperature in the house below 80 for the first time in days and the humidity now hovering somewhere around 10 percent (there was still air being lost through the broken windows), the problems of the world seemed distant, even when they went no farther than his own subdivision.

He finished his coffee, surfed the web on his phone since he no longer needed to conserve battery power for texts and talking with his wife, then put away the dishes, which he washed out over the mulch-covered patio in the backyard. At least he had enough water to wash now. The previous day, Red Cross members had set out a palette of water at the end of the cul-de-sac, no questions asked. He now had fifty gallons of water waiting to be used.

He rummaged in the back of the walk-in pantry, pushing aside Dutch ovens, baking sheets, and steamers until he found what he was looking for: the white box. It was no more than a foot long and three inches deep. Then he walked through the house redirecting extension cords that had been used to power things with the generator. Whistling, he plugged the extension cord into a wall socket in John Clayton's room and climbed the ladder to the Secret Room. The tendrils had thickened almost overnight, turning the Secret Room into a forest jungle of pink, fleshy vines. They had broken through the walls and entered James Howlett's room and even broken through the wall to find the water heater, which they turned into a crumpled mess.

Rylan ignored the damage to his property. It was like a growth. A cancerous growth that was invading his house from the attic outward. All this will soon be over, he thought. There may be nothing I can do about Kaiju Gonzales and nothing I can do about the ribs that are going to destroy my home, but this, this I can fix.

He opened the small white box and removed the electric carving knife. He lined up the blades and inserted them into their slots, then plugged it in.

"Gobble, gobble," he said, smiling at the egg. He placed the electric knife on top of the first tendril that had attached itself to the water heater and pressed the On button. As the blades started sawing back and forth, he felt the kind of satisfactory vengeance that comes from watching hornets fall dying from the nests they build near homeowners' houses. The kind of vengeance that makes a father smile like the Grinch when he hears a mousetrap snapping on a field mouse in the garage. It was vile, yes, but it was getting rid of the pest.

Black crudeness, not unlike oil, bubbled from the tendril, which gave way to the blades easily. Rylan found the tendrils cut as easily as ham. He removed the tendrils from the water heater, then hit the tendrils that had invaded James Howlett's Secret Room and were pushing towards his furniture. There was the dresser, which had a tendril coiled in a drawer like a snake looking for someplace warm to hide. A teddy bear being squeezed by an errant tendril.

Most of the tendrils moved up, however. They branched out to the opening in the roof. These Rylan cut in the middle of the tendril. Gushes of oily liquid poured out. So much so that he grabbed old towels to cover the floor.

"Let's see how long you live without your little feeders," he said to the egg when he was done and most of the tendrils had been cut off and placed in an old iron washbin like the amputated limbs of a giant octopus.

He bathed then in a makeshift shower he had built with the help of his backdoor neighbor. It wasn't fancy, just borrowed sections of broken fence and some gallons of Red Cross jugs connected to a watering can, and there was no way to use soap or shampoo since the drain system was not fixed yet, but it was better than nothing.

The real trick was keeping it unnoticeable from FEMA or the cops. For that, he had to thank a stand of banana trees against his fence line. This meant the shower was technically in his neighbor's yard, but he did not hear them complaining about the fence he was putting in for them, either.

After the shower, he felt prepared to go outside and start working on the fence.

7:21 am

"Ainsley has some family in construction" really translated into "her father owns a construction company." A giant truck full of fence posts, boards, screws, and an industrial auger had pulled up to their house late in the evening. The drivers unloaded enough supplies to rebuild their house, not just their fence. When they left, Ainsley and Lisa's driveway looked like a lumber yard.

Lisa was concerned, of course, that the police would see all this and know that somebody was obviously living there in the quarantine zone.

Since all the families had already marked holes the previous day while they waited for the AC to lower the temperatures in their houses, they just needed to drill out the holes with the auger. Rylan and Lisa manned the auger.

"I feel like I should be the one doing this," Ainsley told her wife. "I'm the one who usually does this type of thing."

"You mean the labor? Well, a. I'm an artist, and this is art, and b. Don't be so stereotypical. Just cause you play with frogs and bugs in the salt marshes doesn't mean I can't handle an auger."

Rylan took one side and Lisa took the other. The trick was making sure the auger went down straight. Ainsley's father had warned Lisa and Ainsley that if the auger went in crooked, it would get stuck in the ground and they would have to dig it up.

The auger cut through the Texas clay like butter, and in less than two minutes, they had a perfectly sized post hole for Amos. Rylan thought back to his days trying to dig through the clay with nothing but a post-hole digger, and just how hard it was to dig through clay.

"Ain't technology grand," he said as they bored out another hole.

One of the problems was that in order to make a hole deep enough, they had to let the auger dig almost to the point where it was covered by its own mud, then pull it back out. And on the fifth hole, it came out crooked and jammed. A painful, sweat-soaked half-hour later, and the auger was finally dug out of the black and brown clay. By the time they finished, Rylan was exhausted. His chest and arms were still sore from his face plant fall on the shingles, and even the pain in his eye was rearing its ugly head.

While they were waiting to start again, Ainsley came out with some lemonade. The smile on her face was grim.

"Got bad news," she said as she handed out glasses of lemonade. "We're being evacuated."

"Bullshit."

"The mayor came on the television and said he was ordering the second evacuation of Houston."

"It's barely been two weeks since Goliad fell," Lisa said.

"Well, sweetie, there isn't much I can do about that. There's another kaiju attack coming."

"We haven't finished putting in the fence."

"I don't' think we'll have to."

They all stood around for a minute, contemplating the threat.

"What do we do?" Ainsley asked her wife.

"We don't leave," Rylan said. "Not yet. This is our property. I'm not relinquishing it to some kaiju."

"You're crazy," Amos said.

"Do you know when Gonzales is expected to make landfall? Don't tell me. If they are evacuating us now, then they must think we have at least three days. Right?"

"Right," Ainsley said.

"That gives us plenty of time to prepare."

"Prepare for what?"

"Protecting our homes. But first, let's finish these postholes."

7:39 am

Solemnity Bay police snuck up on them. While Lisa and Rylan were manning the loud auger, and while Amos was taking a quick pee break from his watch duties, they turned down the street and drove toward Amos' home. Lisa and Rylan were like rabbits spotted in the middle of a football field. There was nowhere they could hide. They would have to drop the auger and run for their homes, and the police would trace them back easily. They were caught.

The cruiser pulled over to the side of the curb, but Rylan and Lisa couldn't stop the auger until it was up and out of the hole. The police waited patiently. Lisa could see the driver radioing something in. Probably that they were about to bring in more people to evacuate.

Amos walked up behind Rylan. Ainsley came from her garage to join them, crossing the lines where fence posts would be buried.

Above them, the teeth-like ribs prepared to snap tight on the survivors. Gotcha!

Rylan recognized the officers as the same people who came around the first time to his house. They were both men in their mid to late twenties, in good physical shape, and well groomed. They were probably new homeowners in Dolphin's Cove or one of the nearby subdivisions, and if their house was not damaged beyond repair, they probably spent their off-duty time working on their homes, just as Rylan and the others were working on theirs.

When Rylan and Lisa finally pulled the auger out of the hole and shut it off, the officer said, "You know you have to evacuate, right?" This was the man who had knocked on Rylan's door a few days ago (though it felt like weeks had passed to Rylan). Officer Grady.

The casual nature of their approach, it suddenly dawned on Rylan. These men weren't going to forcefully evacuate them. That hide-and-seek game was over. At least, to Rylan it was obvious the game was over. By the way that Lisa kept glancing back to her driveway, he could tell she was still worried they would force her and Ainsley to leave.

"We want to get these holes dug first," Amos said. He was still holding his shotgun, but that didn't bother the police. Rylan assumed these officers had met a lot of people with guns over the past few days (he thought specifically of the neighborhood watch guarding Robinson Bayou). They knew the difference between a threat and a casual encounter. This was the latter. If it ever became the former, things would get a whole lot different.

"I understand that. Look, I'm not going to force you to leave," Officer Grady said (and Rylan noted Lisa exhaling deeply then) "because you look like sane and rational people and no sane or rational person would stay here when Kaiju Gonzales appears on their doorstep. As far as I'm concerned, we've been trying to clear this area for over a week now, and still it's full of independent-minded people who have decided to dig in rather than wait and come back. I get it. It's your home. You don't want to abandon it. I wouldn't want to abandon mine. But I want to make sure you're being careful out here. There's worse things than looters and gangs. I want to ask you something. You seen anything really abnormal in the area? And I mean that relative to the giant dead kaiju rotting about a quarter mile that way. Like, a whole other level of weird."

"Why?"

The two police officers looked at each other for a moment like pirates who have been asked about the map to buried treasure. They must have come to a decision about the map and the value of showing it because Officer Grady said, "We're not supposed to talk about this. It is protected intelligence. But the FEMA agents have been talking. They seem to believe the carrion kaiju is coming for a specific reason, something more than eating the corpses of kaiju falls."

"What exactly do you mean?" Amos asked.

"Look, they don't tell us much, but Barry overheard them talking about other monsters in the area, smaller creatures that the carrion kaiju would be lured to. What do you know about angler fish?"

"Are you sure?" Ainsley jumped in.

Her excitement was a little overwhelming for the police officers. "I take it you know about angler fish."

"I am a biologist on the island. I study marine animals, and I have been to a trench before. So yes, I know about anglers." She grabbed Rylan's wrist. "It makes sense."

"What makes sense?" Lisa asked her wife. Rylan and Amos waited for someone to start making some sense.

"You should show them," Ainsley said to Rylan.

"Show us what?"

"The male. I mean, its organ."

"I don't know where you're going with this," Rylan said. "Maybe you can slow down and catch the rest of us up?"

Ainsley's lips curled with the anticipation of a good story. It was a science educator's sneer, the one given to high school students who honestly want to know how a hotdog can freeze that fast in cryogenic fluids.

Delightedly, she said, "Angler fish are small, strange-looking fish from the bottom depths of the ocean. For the longest time, scientists didn't know how they reproduced. They had females, but not males, so maybe, they thought, the fish was asexual. Some of the angler fish they caught they found with these little spikes attached to them, little bumps like brine or a seaweed or something. But then the scientists discovered they were wrong about the attachments on the angler fish. And they also solved the mystery of how the angler fish reproduced. Those tiny bumps were the remains of male angler fish, which are much tinier than female anglers and look kind of like tadpoles. They attach to a female angler and literally become one with the female angler's flesh. The head of the male is consumed, and the rest of its remains begins to pump its reproductive code into the angler, impregnating her. It sounds like Gonzales is a mama angler, and Rylan found a male angler. Show them."

He took the officers to his front lawn and showed them what remained of the creature that had been haunting his house. There was very little left of its corpse. Vultures had gotten to it. Its disjointed legs and/or arms were stripped to the bone, and there was nothing but a small pit in the ground where its belly should have been. The tongue was eaten right out of its mouth like something had been sucking the pimento out of an olive. Its intense eyes were now just two holes in a hollowed-out cavity.

"If you would like to get it off of my lawn, I would greatly appreciate it," Rylan said, spitting. Even with most of the creature gone and a horrible stench from Goliad having settled over the subdivision, the thing stunk awful.

The other officer, Halloran, walked away and said something into his shoulder radio. Officer Grady kneeled down and examined the corpse. "What happened?" he said easily, like they were two buddies at the bar talking about women they'd dated, not about the decomposing corpses of strange, alien creatures. Rylan was impressed at how cool and accepting

Officer Grady was acting, but then again, he supposed that the officers had seen a lot of weird over the past couple of weeks. The bar for weird was probably pretty high. This might not even be the first of these monsters they'd seen.

Rylan told Officer Grady all about the creature lurking in his house, coming in through a hole in his roof. Officer Grady noted the kaiju flesh being used as a tarp and told Rylan that the flesh was "unsanctioned use of kaiju skin" and that he could go to jail for it, but he had done the same thing to his house. "Just make sure it's gone before too long, or if one of them FEMA agents asks to seize it, the answer is 'yes,' and 'whenever you want it.'" Rylan omitted the egg in every way.

"Well, this is not a male organ, I don't believe. You're the scientist," he said to Ainsley, "but I think this looks like one of the parasites I've heard talk about. Now, keep in mind over the past few weeks I've heard a lot of talk about a lot of different things I never knew anything about. Blood fountains, gas sacks, monster semen. But we were also briefed on a number of parasites, and the claws make me think it's one of them. They climb onboard the kaiju, and then fall off when the kaiju falls. They wait for another one to come along like some kind of meat taxi."

"You ever wonder why they say kaiju falls?" Officer Halloran asked. "Nobody says the kaiju died. It's always falls."

Officer Grady snorted with lack of interest. Rylan could tell that Halloran's creative thinking was something Grady had learned to overcome in the short time they were partnered together. "Did you get a van?"

"Yeah. NOAA is on their way."

"Okay. Look, it sometimes takes them awhile, but if you don't want to be picked up by FEMA agents, meaning they see you and call me to forcefully remove you because they are cold heartless Yankee bastards, then I suggest you get inside sometime in the next half hour and stay inside until they're gone."

Rylan nodded and extended his hand. Officer Grady and Halloran shook his hand, and then they shook hands with the other neighbors.

"Remember, please be out before Gonzales arrives. I don't want to see you on national television screaming from your rooftop or running down the street when the kaiju arrives. Remember Biloxi? We're better than that here."

The officers got in their patrol car and drove down the next block.

As soon as the officers disappeared, Lisa turned on Rylan and snapped, "You better have a good plan for the kaiju sex organ you're keeping in your boys' Secret Room."

Amos let out a belch of a laugh that was outwardly loud and singular. He guffawed. "Sorry. That's just the funniest thing I've heard this side of the meat wall. You got any plans for your sex organ, Rylan?"

Lisa chuckled. "Do you think he's compensating for something?"

Rylan smiled. "Okay, get it out."

"Is that a sex organ in your Secret Room, or are you just happy to see me?" Lisa said.

Ainsley, however, did not laugh. She waited while Amos and Lisa laughed. She waited with purpose: arms crossed, eyebrows furrowed. When Amos and Lisa finally stopped snickering, Ainsley said to Rylan, "Despite the laughs, there is a danger to having that thing in our neighborhood. You should have told the police about the organ upstairs. Hell, I should have. I almost did, except it's not my house and we're on good terms. That thing will attract Gonzales, which will bring him to the house across my street. We have to remove it."

"Okay, after NOAA leaves, bring every saw, kitchen knife, and shovel you have, and we will cut the thing out. Then we can drive it far away from here and dump it where there aren't any buildings."

They returned to their homes and sat by the blinds and waited for NOAA to collect the body.

The police were wrong about one thing. They had to wait most of the rest of the day for NOAA to show up. It wasn't until after Goliad's ribs were casting long shadows across the Galveston Bay that a NOAA van showed up. The white van was covered, like so much else, in a thick patina of dust and dirt kicked up by the kaiju fall. Somebody wrote with their finger in the dirt: I WISH MY WIFE WAS THIS DIRTY

They removed the corpse in pieces, and each piece was placed in a separate bag. The bags were tagged and placed in containers in the van. Then one of the agents knocked on Rylan's front door. The agent knocked twice more, then left a hanging informational packet on the knob of his door. They finished packing and sprayed some chemicals where the kaiju parasite had lain (Rylan was sure it would kill his grass). Then they drove away.

6:50 pm

In the Secret Room, the four stood on the landing. They had brought a tarp and rope to help maneuver the organ. They were all wearing safety glasses. While Rylan only had his electric carving knife, Lisa brought over a chainsaw, and Amos had not one, but two machetes.

"What's the second machete for?" Rylan asked.

"Nothing wrong with overkill. So is the plan to cut this thing out?"

"Yes, but…" Things had changed in the twelve hours since he was up there. He remembered taking the carving knife to the long tentacles. The amputated parts were still in the iron washbin, and the water heater still looked like something the Hulk had played with. But the organ had shot new tentacles out of its main body, and the tentacles that were only partly severed had sprouted new tentacles like branches from a cut tree limb.

"This is amazing." Ainsley awed at the number of tentacles as she scanned the room.

"It is a disaster," Rylan said. "I spent almost an hour this morning hacking off limbs, and they've either grown back or been absorbed."

"There is a lot of study into the nervous system of octopus legs and the behavior surrounding them. For instance, did you know that octopuses are cannibalistic? Yet when presented with a tank of severed limbs, including their own severed limbs, the octopus will not eat its own limbs."

"Great. Fascinating. Can we get this thing out of here?"

"What's the plan, man?" Amos asked.

"The plan is to cut this fucker out of my house using any means necessary, and trying to do as little damage to my kids' play room as possible. Then, we haul it out on the tarp, put in the truck, and drop it at the bottom of Dickinson bayou, far away from most people's homes. Then we get out of here before Gonzales makes landfall."

"Current estimates are two days, maybe three," Lisa said. She had become the group's go-to source for Kaiju Gonzales information.

"Alright then," Amos said. "Let's gut this thing." In one quick movement, he chopped off a two-inch-thick cord of kaiju meat, severing it completely. The machete stuck in the floorboard.

"Oh, this is going to be fun," Amos said, realizing how soft the shoots were.

"Be wary of the body. A couple of days ago when I was up here shooting the parasite monster thing, I took a couple of shots at this piece of horrible, and the bullets did nothing. In fact, it spit the lead out. Here," he said, and picked up the mashed bullet from the floorboard to show them the result.

"Amazing," Ainsley said.

Lisa said, "Of course you would find that amazing. You're so weird. I love you." She placed her arms around Ainsley's neck and pecked her on the lips. Then the harvesting of tentacles really began.

Rylan used his electric carving knife for the thinnest tentacles, and Amos hacked at the medium sized ones. Ainsley took the chainsaw to the thickest members. Once all the tentacles were severed, they tried pushing the organ. It still wouldn't budget.

"I hate to tell you this, but if those tentacles went left, right, and up, they probably went down, too," Ainsley said.

Lisa and Rylan stood to either side of the body and lifted it up as much as possible while Ainsley fired up the chainsaw and dug into the flesh like she was ripping out overgrown weeds. It cut slowly. Bits of flesh flung everywhere. Lisa was glad she had chosen the old overalls for this work. There would be no getting the stink out.

Eventually, Ainsley cut through the tentacles/stalks with a final RRIIIPP. The body, which had turned a blue/purple/black color that was somehow darker than its usual color, could be rolled onto the tarp. Lisa and Ainsley lowered the body down through the hole in the Secret Room to Rylan and Amos, who had to twist the kaiju body part sideways without smacking into the walls or getting blood on the carpet.

As they began dragging the mass of flesh across the den, though, they heard familiar voices outside.

"Shit, shit, shit," Rylan said. "Why does this keep happening to me?" He wished they had the chainsaw they had left up in the Secret Room.

"Hey, boy, we coming for you," cooed the thief with the shaved head. By the sound of it, there were at least five men with him. They didn't even knock this time, just kicked the door in and started knocking over furniture.

"Where you hiding, you poker-carrying son of a bitch?" called out the man with the bleached ponytail.

As his eye tingled with ghost pain, Rylan reached for the gun tucked in the back of his jeans.

Ainsley grabbed his hand. "No," she said in a hushed voice. "The goal is to get this thing out of your house. They'll overturn some furniture, break another of your many broken windows, and probably steal your television, but it won't be anything that can't be replaced by insurance, especially after a kaiju attack. None of it is worth risking your life or your house for. We can lower this thing out into your backyard. Then I will bring the pickup around, and we can take off from there."

Rylan nodded. He hated allowing thieves to burglarize his home. In a way, it was like letting them kick his head again. He was glad to have friends who were thinking with their heads rather than their pride. Ainsley's plan made good sense, assuming the thieves didn't open the back patio door. He had to keep thinking of the main goal and not get sidetracked by hooligans. And moving around the backyard was actually a great idea since the fence wasn't up yet.

They tied the ropes through the loopholes in the tarp and gently, slowly, scooted the mass out the back window and onto the back patio overlook. Rylan heard a crash from downstairs.

"Help them," Amos told Rylan. He pulled a Beretta out of his boot and walked quietly to the side of the stairs. Rylan wondered how many guns Amos owned. Every time the dude came around, he had a new gun.

Ainsley climbed down the patio railing. Their house had almost the exact same build as Rylan's house, so they knew that the looters wouldn't see her if she went down the far side of the patio. Once she was down, Lisa and Rylan started lowering the mass. It went gently at first. About halfway down, Lisa started to lose her grip, and Rylan had to reach over and grab the rope before she dropped it. Now he was lowering the kaiju organ completely on his own. It was much more weight than he was used to. Rylan was a decently fit guy. No gym rat, but he could bench 180 without needing a spotter. This mass was easily 250 pounds, though. It took the exertion of all his muscles to not drop it onto the patio.

To his side, Lisa inhaled sharply. She was looking back towards the staircase, where a shadow was ascending. Rylan felt trapped. With no options, he kept lowering the fleshy egg-like organ and hoped that he wouldn't get killed.

The man with the shadow crept up the staircase, a gun in one hand and the flame-tongued bat from downstairs in the other. The fingers of a dragon tattoo clawed at his neck. Just as he was about to shout something to the others, Amos cleared his throat and put the Beretta to the man's handkerchief-covered head.

"Not a word," Amos said, then motioned to come aside. As the man came near, Amos took the man's gun and the bat and gave them both to Lisa.

"Sit against the wall where I can see you. Cross your legs, hands on the ground. Put that hanky-covered skull of yours on the floor." Amos glared at the thug with that weird sideways look to him. The thug decided to do just as he was told.

Rylan continued to lower the kaiju body part. Sweat broke out in fat beads on his forearms and his head. He arched his back to move the weight to his legs.

"Look at this," somebody said from downstairs. Rylan was pretty sure it was the ponytail guy. "Dude's got him jungle lovin' for a wife." There was another crash. The picture frame? Had they found the wedding photo? And the certificates?

"Ignore him," Lisa said.

The hooligan under Amos' gun sneered from underneath his low-hanging handkerchief. Rylan glared.

"This is a Beretta," Amos said. "It is a small gun by Magnum standards, but it is powerful enough to turn your head into a red smear on that wall. And with y'all barging into this man's house amidst all the chaos of the kaiju fall, no cop would prosecute me. Hell, I doubt they'd investigate. So go ahead and scoff again. I'd love to make a Rorschach out of your brains."

Rylan felt tension give out on the rope. The body part was on the ground.

"You go down first," Amos said. "Then Lisa, then scumdog here."

"We're taking him with us?" Lisa asked.

"If he plays nice, we'll let him out at the corner of the Cove."

Rylan started down the patio railing. Ainsley had already taken off for the pickup, staying low to the ground so as not to be seen. Lisa quickly came down after Rylan. Then came the Hispanic gang member slow as a soccer player being subbed out of a game that his team was trying to preserve a win. As soon as he hit the floor, Rylan pulled the Glock on him.

More crashing came from inside.

"Boy, they are fucking yo place up," the gangbanger said to Rylan.

"Don't listen to him. He's a dumbass," Amos said as he came down the railing. "He doesn't know how close to dying he is."

"Drop your guns," a voice said from around the corner of the house. Rylan looked and saw a giant man roughly the size of Leatherface with his massive hand around the back of Ainsley's neck. She stood next to Leatherface as rigid as rebar on a cold night. The man had a TEC-9 pointed to Ainsley's chest.

Rylan dropped the Glock, then Amos reluctantly dropped the Beretta. The tall gangbanger picked them up, laughing.

"The machete, too."

Amos put down his machete. The gangbanger with the dragon claws tattoo and the low-hanging handkerchief picked up the machete, then took a few practice swings at Amos' neck. "I should go all Crazy Arab on you. Who's the dumbass now?"

"Take whatever you want and leave," Rylan said.

"Y'all's the ones we're after," Leatherface said. "This ain't about stealing. This is retribution. You beat up a couple of my warriors. Mis hermanos guerras. Now we're going to destroy everything you own. Make an example of you to everyone else."

By then, the other gangbangers had come out of the house. The man with the ponytail had Rylan's wedding photo and certificate in his hand.

Seeing Rylan, he stuffed the photo and the certificate down his front pocket.

"What do you want to do, Tramposo?" the man with the ponytail asked their leader. Tramposo had long brushy hair and a beard that would make the loudest Southern Rock bands proud. He was dressed in black except for a white bandana with a green and red cross on it.

"I want to light up this asshole's house, and then I want to light up the homes of these other assholes. I want to remind these people that the streets belong to the Cruces."

The Los Cruces cheered. Rylan, Lisa, and Amos were forced to sit down next to the house while the gang started a fire on his back patio. They started with some lumber in his fire pit, but as the fire outgrew the fire pit, they expanded it by using broken bits of Rylan's furniture and other boards. By then, the sun had set.

"That's my house," Rylan pleaded to Tramposo. "Don't destroy my house. I raised my boys here. We buried our first dog in the backyard not far from where you're standing. C'mon. Don't light up my house. Kick my face in again if it makes you feel better, but please leave my home alone."

The giant man listened to Rylan. In the dark, his face glowed from the light of dancing embers.

"I feel for you. I used to have a home myself. But you got to learn that it ain't nothing more than walls and a roof. Nothing more than timber and nails holds it together. Pinche guey."

"You're wrong. There's more to it than that. There's the history of the house. It isn't just lumber and nails. That place you want to burn is literally the history of me and my family. We didn't just sleep there. We lived there. It is our history you are hell-bent on destroying. And it's love that holds it together."

"Love and history? Shit, what about the love of my warriors. We stick together. One tribe. And history? You assaulted my brothers. What about that history?"

"They assaulted me."

Tramposo leaned in close and spoke in a quiet whisper.

"And now you must be punished. And more importantly, I must make sure that nobody ever tries to assault my family again. So see, this has to happen. Your history, your love? It's going to have to survive the fire."

"No!"

While Tramposo turned his back to him, Rylan leaped to his feet. Because the fire, which was now a small bonfire, was between him and the other gang members, they didn't see what Rylan was doing until it was too late. Rylan reached down and grabbed a fire log, a leg from the dining table his family ate at, and before anyone could react, he cold-cocked Tramposo. Tramposo went down like high timber in East Texas. Problem was, he fell face-forward into the fire. His brothers rushed to his help while Rylan swung at the closest man to him. It happened to be the guy with the bleached ponytail, the one with his wedding photo. Rylan really wanted to make this hit count. He hit him in the kidneys hard enough to drop him. As the man arched his back, Rylan kicked him in the stomach. Then he reached into the guy's pocket and took his redshirt wedding photo and certificate back. He unfolded the crumpled certificate in his hands. The lipstick shined like a red wax on a king's ransom. He punched ponytail once more, this time hard enough to split a tooth and cut his lip.

To his side, Amos and Lisa had picked up their own sticks and were attacking a gang member. But by then, guns had been pulled. The hooligan with the low-hanging handkerchief jabbed Amos' Beretta in his side. They dropped the sticks.

They were surrounded by Los Cruces gang members with loaded guns aimed at them. As the other gangbangers helped Tramposo up, Tramposo's beard was smoking. The air stunk of singed hair. One of the gang members tried to pat the burn with his handkerchief. Tramposo punched him.

"Kill him! Kill that mother fucker!" He pointed at Rylan.

Guns cocked in the firelight. The sound had an electrical effect on Rylan, like a click going off in his head and a gear shifting in his soul. The gear was something he always had there, waiting for the right moment to kick in. It was a gear of inevitability, of Rylan coming to grips with the reality that he might never see another sunrise, never kiss his wife, or hug his children. Once that gear took effect, choices were limited and everything was possible.

From out in the dark, more guns cocked.

Into the light stepped a horde of Rylan's neighbors. They were a microcosm of the people who lived in the area. There were people brandishing guns, bats, machetes, tillers, and any other handed weapon. There were old people with muttonchops and squirrel killers, first-generation immigrants with baseball bats, NASA engineers with chainsaws and boards with nails in them, and a couple of people with nothing more than their fists. Some of his neighbors who clearly were hunters had Remingtons and Winchesters with hunting scopes. Mrs. Agnew had her leggings and her headscarf and a Magnum. At the front of them, Rylan recognized Jim and Christine Dao. They had returned. Jim was holding a 9-inch, curved fisherman's knife. Rylan thought of the damage he had seen a pair of scissors do in Jim's skilled hands.

"This is our subdivision," Jim said. "These are our homes. I know you are looking at me and think you are seeing just an old man. But let me tell you. I am an old man with nothing left but his home. If I lose it, you might as well kill me."

"I see a man with a knife," Tramposo said. "You think I'm scared of a knife fight?"

"No, but I've cut up thousands of fish with this knife. I can split a Redfish from ass to gills in one cut with this knife. What you think I can do to you?"

Tramposo lunged at Jim. Jim ducked easily and swiped his blade across Tramposo's stomach. Tramposo stumbled backwards. A wet line emerged from his shirt.

"I wasn't even trying," Jim said. "Next time, I will cut you deeper."

"There's only six of you and there's at least twenty of us," Rylan said. "You are younger and stronger, but we're older and wiser. And more desperate. Mrs. Agnew called the cops ten minutes ago. They'll be here any minute. Get out now. If we see you again, it will be the last time."

The gangbangers looked at each other and to their leader. Tramposo's skin was blistering on one side of his face. He spat on the ground and backed away. His gang followed him.

"Leave the weapons," Amos said. The gangbangers tossed their guns on the grass as they ran out of the Cove.

Rylan hugged Jim and Christine and thanked them. Then they all started walking among their neighbors and shaking hands and hugging. A lot of people were saying that if he needed anything, to let them know. The fire was put out.

"How did you get back?" Rylan asked Jim.

"Nobody cares about incoming traffic anymore. They switched the lanes at I-45 and only care about evacuation now that everybody is trying to leave again."

"You came just in time. Thank you."

"That was the easy part," Jim said once they were alone. "The hard part is still out in the Gulf."

"Yeah, but I've got an idea for that," Rylan said. "First things first, we've got to dump this kaiju thing."

"The egg?" Christine asked. "Why?"

"It's not an egg. It's a sex organ. Kaiju sex organ," Amos said.

"What?" Jim wrinkled his nose.

"Like some deep-dwelling fish," Lisa added. "We learned that from the authorities."

"Doesn't sound like any fish I've ever caught," Jim said. His wife said something encouraging to him in Vietnamese, and Jim nodded. "There are some funky fish out there, though. Is Kaiju Gonzales after the organ?"

"Yes. At least, that's what we think is attracting it here. We can't be for sure, but there is too much risk."

Ainsley said, "No, we're pretty sure about it. He may not be, but I am. The more I look at it, yeah, it's a reproductive organ."

"What do you mean?" Rylan asked.

"Well, if you want to go into biology 101, there's some basic components of most male sex organs. Components like a sack to hold the genetic material. There is also a depositor."

"She means penis," Lisa said.

"Depositor," Ainsley intoned. She went to the organ and pointed to a long flap of skin that peeled backward. "I think this is the depositor."

The men in the group stammered.

"We have to be careful," Ainsley said. "Like a tiny male angler fish, this thing is very much alive. It is already sending out shooters. I think it is taking much of its nourishment from the humidity, which would make sense if it came from a water environment like the deep sea."

With everyone grabbing a hold of the tarp, they leveraged the organ into the back of Rylan's pickup. Everyone except Rylan stayed in the back with the organ to make sure its little tendrils didn't branch off into the truck.

Despite Lisa's warnings, the organ never branched out. It was like it knew what was happening. Under the dark of night, they dumped the organ, tarp and all, into the Dickinson bayou. It fell in, its black flesh turning pink again, then flesh-toned. The black bayou water overwhelmed the organ, and it disappeared into the dark. Once the organ was completely submerged, Amos pulled out a flask and shared it around.

Behind them loomed the giant face of Kaiju Goliad. Lisa picked up a rock and chunked it at the mostly-still-covered-in-flesh head. Half an eyeball floated in one eye socket, leering at them with an undead gaze. The rock fell hopelessly far short of the head, which lay miles away.

"Hey, who wants to climb it?" Ainsley said in the dark.

9:12 pm

The climb had not been as hard as Rylan thought. NOAA handrails had been inserted into the kaiju's neck to help with ascending. At first they took the path that led into the kaiju's head through one of its eye holes. A raised gangplank had been built to help agents walk across the eye socket without slipping in intravenous fluid. The gangplank ended in a large hole.

"Anybody want to see a kaiju's brain?" Ainsley teased. She shined her flashlight into the skull.

The brain was a labyrinth of large, grey loops. Squiggles, Rylan thought. But the stench was too powerful for anyone to stay inside the eye socket any longer, so they retreated and took the higher climb, which led them to the top of Daikaiju Goliad's upturned jaw.

Behind them, the kaiju's vertebra rose into the sky. Mechanical zip lines had been bolted to the bone to help NOAA agents move around the fall.

Dickinson bayou lay ahead of them like spilled ink on a black canvas. The Gulf wind blew in their faces, bringing with it that briny, salt smell. Like oysters and shrimp and all the creatures that were fished from its waters.

"I wanted to ask you about kaiju skin, but we haven't had the chance," Rylan said to Ainsley.

"Been fighting off giant worms, kaiju parasites, and gangs. I understand. Kaiju skin is a very thin, soft shell layered over dense epidermal cells. The shell is more like a layer of mucus, but not as gooey and sticky. More like wax."

"It's like her," Lisa said. "A soft outer veneer – 'Ainsley' – covering this tough, 'I only work in the fields' biologist."

Rylan chuckled. They sat down on the edge of Goliad's jaw. Rylan watched his feet dangle over the edge. The flask of whisky was passed around again.

"I supposed we leave now," Amos said. "Two days from landfall, and after tonight I don't think many robbers will be trying to get into the Cove." He paused, then said, "Problem is, I don't want to leave."

"Why not?" Jim asked. "It's not like you are old people like me and Christine with nothing to gain from leaving. Just give us some beer and pho, and we will be just fine. Why would you stay?"

"I guess pride, maybe. You know I was born premature? This was at a time before neonatal care wards. All my parents could do was wait and hope. But my daddy said I was too stubborn. Too proud to die. Like just existing was my middle finger to the universe. I guess that's stuck with me all my life. Hell, it was in me before I was born. My bloodline runs straight to the Alamo. So in a way, I'm always up for a last stand."

Lisa said, "Ainsley and I have fought all our adult lives for acceptance. Our life together, our marriage, it isn't recognized by the state of Texas. But our home ownership is recognized. We own the property together. I don't know how much longer we'll be here before the kaiju comes ashore, but we're not going down without a fight either."

"What about you, Rylan?" Christine asked. "For the rest of us, this is all we have. You have a family and children. Why do you stay?"

The others waited. Rylan watched the bayou and the bay beyond.

"I was eleven when we lost our home. I was playing Super Mario Brothers. Suddenly, the tornado warning sirens went off, and my mother and father grabbed me and took me to the basement. We were in the basement maybe a minute before the tornado hit. I don't know for sure. It was a long time ago. Some things get distorted. Your memory fucks with itself. But some things I remember clear as yesterday. Like how the basement smelled like dust. And I remember the noise. It was so loud, you couldn't hear your thoughts. When we came out, the house was as gone as Dorothy's prairie home in Kansas. There was crap strewn everywhere, but the house was gone. There was this deer I found. I thought it was dead, but it jumped up while I was petting it. I saw a lot of strange and horrible things that day, things I don't talk about to anyone who isn't God. It took us a year to recover. My parents lost their home and their business. We slept on cots in a high school gym for a week, then we were moved to FEMA trailers. Eventually, my parents had to sell the house for a loss. Those were some really dark days."

"Oh my God," Lisa said. "I had no idea."

"On the plus side, I've been into building things ever since. I first used a saw and hammer – I mean really used them – helping other people rebuild their homes after the tornado. It helped make everything easier. Eventually I got into engineering, and now here I am. Today I nearly lost my home to one kind of invader. I'm not going to lose it to another."

"What do you mean?" Ainsley asked.

"I think I can stop this thing."

"The military has a hard time fighting off kaiju. They don't stop them, they only divert them. What makes you think you can do something the military can't?"

"They can't stop kaiju cause they're fighting a military target, and Gonzales is not a military target."

"What kind is she?"

"She's an oil and gas problem. I can stop her if I have the right supplies."

+17 DAYS

8:51 am

Rylan woke up to texts from his wife.

"Where the hell r you?"

"Text me pls!"

"IF YOU DNT TXT ME THIS MORNING, IM GOING TO ASSUME SOMETHING REALLY REALLY BAD AND CALL THE POLICE"

"Shit," he groaned as he dropped the phone.

"I'm ok," he texted back. "Sry"

She FaceTimed him directly then, and it was time to confess. He told her about the parasite that had been creeping around his house so he had to kill it. He told her about the men in the gang who jumped him but how his neighbors had fought them off, but then the whole gang came back and tried to burn the house down, except this time Jim and Christine and the whole damn neighborhood was there to stop them. When she asked if there was anything else, he told her about the thing in the Secret Room that they thought was an egg but really was a reproductive organ that they had to dump in the bayou.

"Rylan, I want to make this clear. You are going to get in the truck, and you are coming to Austin to be with your family."

"I can't. I have to do something."

"I don't know why I don't just hang up on you. Listen to me. What can possibly be more important than your wife and children, Rylan? We are here. We need you. Alive."

"Last night I grabbed our wedding photo and name change certificates out of some degenerate's pocket, and then I punched him so hard I broke his teeth. I did this for paper, Tamara. And I got to thinking that it's not the memory of us that he was stealing. We have that photo backed up on a hard drive in Austin and on a cloud somewhere. So it isn't the memory of it. And it isn't the moment itself because nobody can take that away from us, right? That's our moment. It's the symbol. It's what stealing our photos represents. It's like he's stealing a part of us. And for the past three weeks, everyone's been taking from us. Our home, our possessions, our life. I'm tired of letting the world take everything we've built up, Tamara, and I won't take it anymore. I've got a plan. I know how to kill Kaiju Gonzales, and with the help of some of our neighbors, I'm going to do it."

"Nobody's taken down a kaiju. Not even the military, Rylan. Don't lose it, baby. Focus on what matters."

"I've never been more focused. I can do this. Trust me. I can do this."

"Can't you just tell the military your bright plan and let them do it for you?"

"You remember when Tatanka was working that DOD contract on a new drillbit for sand? We had this great idea that we knew would help. They're still working the kinks out of it, and that was an idea pitched by a company years ago, not some petro engineer. Some ideas have to be forged in the fire."

She covered her hand over her face. "I don't want you to do this."

"I have to do this. For you. For John Clayton and James Howlett. You still love me?"

She looked away. "Yes, I still love you."

"For better or for worse?"

"Feels like a whole lot worse right now, so it better be better quick, Rylan. I love you. I can't believe I'm saying this. Stay safe, and if it gets bad, please, please, please get the hell out of there."

By the time he hung up, police were driving through the streets blaring their sirens and trying to make life completely miserable for anyone remaining in the neighborhood. Something must have changed.

"Solemnity Bay is under mandatory evacuation. There is a 90 percent probability rate for a direct attack from Kaiju Gonzales. You must leave immediately. This will be a militarized zone under full military law. Anyone in the militarized zone after 5 pm tonight will be handled by the military. You will be treated as a trespasser in a military operation."

Rylan remembered that when he left Solemnity Bay the first time, the probability for a direct hit was seventy percent. He closed the window curtains and went back to doing his laundry. (At least with the washer running, it drowned out the sound of the sirens.)

He ate breakfast. Oatmeal because he could microwave it. After breakfast, he switched the laundry out. Then he took a long Red Cross bath in the tub. (He heated the water on the stove first.) He wasn't sure if or when he'd have another chance to bathe, so he decided to risk it and hope that the water could drain. It did. When the bath was finished and he had dried off, he walked downstairs to fetch warm underwear right out of the dryer. There was a fresh goodness about clothes right out of the dryer.

Once dressed, he opened the door and picked up the mess of flyers that lay strewn about his porch like the colorful feathers of a paper turkey.

"At least I won't be seeing you guys for a while," he said. He dumped the advertising in the garbage bag that was already full of flyers, business cards, brochures, and quotes. He crossed in front of a neighbor who had loaded their car up (again) and was evacuating Solemnity Bay. He tossed the garbage bag into the debris pile that was now the size of a small Crossover. Then he went to Amos, who was already up and waiting. The man opened the door before Rylan could knock. They went to Lisa and Ainsley's home. Lisa and Ainsley were in their garage, making plans of some kind.

"Last night, I got to thinking about biophobias," Ainsley said. To Rylan's scrunched-up face, she said, "Biophobias are natural things in the environment that make you want to avoid a place. Think the dark woods versus the lighted path. They are natural, some think even genetic, tendencies built into human evolution. But we also find the same kind of markers throughout the animal kingdom. One of the strongest is the repulsion of stripes. Stripes are a way for animals to communicate to other animals that they are poisonous or highly toxic. Wasps, snakes, even fish all employ the same basic pattern. The pattern is so powerful that other animals use it to be pseudo-wasps and false rattlesnakes. They pretend to be a venomous animal so that other animals will leave them alone."

"Red and black, okay Jack," Amos said.

"Exactly. I want to do the same thing. I want to make bold stripes on our roads. I think it will force Kaiju Gonzales to go where we want, at least for a little while. If we're lucky, it might even force it away."

"Nice," Rylan said.

"Well, I started thinking like you, that maybe if I considered Gonzales as a purely biological target, maybe I could come up with a solution. What's yours?"

Rylan told them the plan. It would be risky and take most of the day to gather the supplies, but he thought he could do it with their support. While Ainsley and Lisa worked with Ainsley's father to gather paint for the roads, he would go out and gather the supplies he needed.

After hearing the plan, Amos said, "We're screwed."

"That might be the dumbest idea I've ever heard," Ainsley added.

"Dreams in the Dinosaur," Rylan said, a glint of something impish in his smile. .

"What is that? What is 'Dreams in the Dinosaur?'"

"When I was younger and dumber, I went clubbing with my buddies. Westheimer, Kirby Road, Montrose, better or worse, we hit them all. And one time we were at this club with this giant, garish monster standing in the middle of the dance floor. It had laser lights coming out of its plastic body and a disco ball hanging from its mouth like a shiny, mirror-balled tongue. I think it was supposed to be a T-rex but ended up more like Godzilla with really long arms. And standing beneath this dinosaurian creature, of course, is a beautiful black woman who I'd one day call my bride. There are these other guys coming up to her, and she just brushes them off. But I've got to give it a shot. So I go up to her, and I say probably the worst thing you can say."

"You said 'you had a dream' to her," Ainsley said.

"'I have a dream, and the dream is you,' to be exact. She should have slapped me, but by the grace of God, she didn't. She told me I needed to get some new lines that weren't racially sensitive. She spent the next twenty minutes schooling me on race issues, but I was just glad she was talking to me. When she was done, I asked for her number. She told me to go to hell. I think there were a lot more cuss words when said it, though. She walked off, and I thought I'd never see her again. I went to the Dancing Dinosaur every night for a week hoping to catch her, but she never showed. About three months later I was at this conference for Fluid Dynamics, though, and I was going to go home. I wasn't feeling well. Can't remember why. But I dived into this ultra-boring seminar, I think because there were a lot of empty seats and I could kind of crumple over without being seen by anyone. And I heard this voice. It was high-pitched with a little of drawl to it. I knew it was her. She was the last speaker in the presentation, so when she finished, I asked if she knew anything about dinosaur hunting strategies. She told me dinosaurs had nothing to do with the presentation. But she was smiling. So I told her I'd take that as a no and educate her. I told her that some dinosaurs, such as the Sinocalliopteryx, were ambush predators. They would lie in wait for their prey to make an appearance somewhere, and then they would ask them out for a date. She said yes that time. Sometimes the dumbest ideas have the biggest pay-offs."

9:13 am

Lisa took the wheel of the Suburban. They were leaving for the paint and rollers, which were at a warehouse. The side door creaked as Ainsley opened it. Her voice creaked as she talked to Rylan.

"There are two kinds of kaiju, Rylan. Kaiju and the super-sized daikaiju. But when you are out there, keep in mind that there are two other ways that NOAA classifies kaiju. Shinda kaiju, like Kaiju Goliad, are dead kaiju. Fallen. Kaiju Gonzales has a different classification. Kui kaiju. Devourers. Kui kaiju behave differently than shinda kaiju."

Rylan thought of the lamprey that had attacked them on the roads. He couldn't agree with Ainsley more. Kui kaiju act differently.

"They aren't just frustrated, psycho-crazy kaiju. They have a purpose. Kaiju Gonzales' purpose is breeding and devouring. She won't be easily swayed. If I don't see you before your crazy mining expedition, I wanted to say that I am really proud of you. Most people talk about standing up to the kaiju and doing something about it, but you really are."

"*We* really are, Ainsley. Take care of Lisa. Good luck with the biophobia."

"I want to call this Battlefield: Clear Lake. This is going to be pretty awesome, right?"

They hugged, then Ainsley climbed into the Suburban, and they drove out of the subdivision.

Rylan called an old college friend, Mike Crenshaw, to ask for some welding work.

"You're lucky you caught me," Mike said. "I can do that for you, no problemo. Got the parts and everything. Better be quick, though. I'm leaving today, no matter what."

Amos followed Rylan to the garage, where he made sure the truck bed was empty except for tarps and bolt cutters, then they drove out of the Cove. A bunch of news crews had set up outside the "Come and Take It" sign hanging from the subdivision's walls. They focused on the sign and on the cars evacuating for a second time in as many weeks.

Leaving the Clear Lake area was easy. They followed the caravan out and received little more than dirty looks from state troopers who had been rooting out inhabitants for the past week. They drove across the Egret Bay Bridge without being stopped or asked for identification and entered a world that was being evacuated. Most lanes were outgoing, and Rylan feared an outbound lane would force them out of Houston.

"If we don't get out of here, we may not have a chance to turn around until Huntsville."

Rylan hopped over a curb and cut through a parking lot to get into the one lane going east toward the bay and 146. They drove down around the actual Clear Lake and saw the gargantuan beast rotting on the far side, where they lived. Most of its tail was reduced to bones and the water around the tail had turned red. Beams were being erected to keep the vertebra from shifting in the soft ground.

"In ten years, it will be like Stonehenge," Rylan said.

"Kaiju-henge?" Amos offered. "You know, there's already a cult that worships Kaiju Pearl in New Orleans. Maybe some cult will appear and worship Goliad."

"You could lead that cult."

Amos smiled. "I know I come across as a little odd. It's the eyes, mostly, I think. Never got them corrected. And I like my guns."

"Me, too."

"I thought you didn't have any."

"None you can fire."

"So you have replicas?"

"Not exactly. You know Star Trek?"

"Very well."

"At home I have three Phaser-1 replicas from TOS. I got one of them signed by George Takei. I prefer them to the Next Generation phasers because they look more like weapons."

"TNG changed them to these things that look like remote controls. I never liked them."

"When this is all over, I have a Phaser-3 replica rifle from The Original Series. It's up in Austin right now, but once we move back, you should come by and take a look."

They drove east toward 146 and passed an electronic billboard reminding them *Hurricane Season is Here. Always be prepared.* They couldn't make it much farther than Clear Lake Park. Goliad had entered Clear Lake here. He had dragged himself across the land, creating a small canyon, before he entered the muddy water. Even if they could have made it to the state road, it was completely blocked off for military use. Convoys of 5-ton trucks with canvas tops passed them. Explosives ordinance signs were mounted to the sides of some of the trucks. For every 5-ton, there was at least one more Humvee and an additional MRAP. The MRAPs, tall, v-shaped trucks with remote weapons systems on top, were intimidating. In the distance, the ribcage of Goliad lay like a hollowed-out mountain on the coast.

Rylan turned his vehicle around. He wound his way down Space Center Boulevard, which took him past the Johnson Space Center, then subdivisions that were pulverized by Goliad's retreat.

"For lack of a better word, the destruction here is awesome," Amos said as he gazed out his window. "I thought we had it bad in Solemnity Bay, but we're at the kaiju's grave. Here, Goliad fought. My God, it's like everything is gone."

Rylan couldn't look at the ruins without feeling a pang in his heart. The area was flattened. There were not even trees anymore. He remembered driving down this road less than a month ago. The area was all Nature Preserve butted up against subdivisions. He couldn't see ten feet off the road because of all the trees and houses. Now, he could see clear to the state road.

NASA's Neutral Buoyancy Laboratory was preserved, and Ellington Air Force Base survived Goliad, too. This was a good thing because it was now the staging ground for all military activities in the area, which meant that soldiers with dogs were now patrolling its fence line. Rylan made sure not to slow down. The fields at Ellington were covered with more military helicopters than he had ever seen in his life. Every open space seemed to be filled with Black Hawks, Chinooks, and Apaches.

"Look at all that firepower. They are going to blast that son of a bitch into kingdom come, Rylan. Makes you wonder what a couple of stooges like us can do in light of all that weaponry."

Amos sat back and took it all in: the destruction on one hand, the military response on the other. "I don't know where I live anymore. I thought I lived in a quiet, middle-class subdivision outside of Houston in a little-known town of less than two thousand people. Now, I feel like I live in a war zone. This looks as bombed to hell as any Middle Eastern city I've ever seen on television."

None of it compared to what lay ahead of them, however. North of Ellington Field, they ran into massive amounts of destruction, the likes they had never seen before. This was where Kaiju Goliad had retreated from the military stand next to the refineries. Kaiju Goliad had run straight through the city of South Houston, Texas.

Rylan had gone to school at Texas Tech and so lived on the flat, flat Texas plains for four years of his life. The people who lived there were called flatlanders because the land there was a like a line on a horizon that disappeared in the distance. This part of South Houston was normally a mismatch of industrial and residential buildings. It was not uncommon to see signs advertising hard hat safety equipment and pipe rigging along the highways. But all of it was gone. Not vanished, but reduced to that flat line on the horizon.

Rylan stopped the car and they both got out and faced the razed world.

"I thought I knew what the word carnage meant," Amos said. "This part of the world has been erased, Rylan. There's nothing left. I must have watched every giant monster movie from the fifties to the seventies. But none of it is relevant to what I see now."

The pickup came to a gaping hole in the road. This was Goliad's path. They drove off the road and onto the city's ruins. They felt dirty, like they were plowing over the bones of the dead. The road was slow with the worry of hidden nails and broken glass.

They stopped to eat lunch in the shadow of a storage tank that had survived Goliad's massacre. Along the side of the tank was a long mural half the length of a football field. The mural depicted Texans carrying rifles and pulling a canon towards the battlefield at San Jacinto, which was not far from them. They ate chips and peanut butter sandwiches.

12:53 pm

After lunch, they started down the highway where Goliad had been turned around. The drive was clear as Rylan drove to the Tatanka Oil equipment lot. Next to the lot was the building for Tatanka Oil. A large gash radiated outward from the corner of one side of the building. He wondered what caused the damage. The tip of Goliad's tail? Maybe shrapnel from the battle struck the building. It was unsafe to enter, whatever the cause, and was roped off. The equipment lot, however, stood outside of the roped area.

He had the code to open the lock to the equipment lock and get inside. (He always wondered why a simple tumbler lock was all that stood between thieves and millions of dollars of equipment.) He loaded a drill bit, piping, and a drive.

The drive out of the destruction was much easier. They knew the way and where to avoid footprints. On the way back, they stopped at the Home Surplus. The lines were gone, as were most of the store's products. Rylan bought some more parts and then drove back into Clear Lake. A state trooper stopped his truck to remind him to get the hell out of town, that they were under military evacuation, and if he saw him again, he didn't care where Rylan lived, he would force him to move, at gunpoint if necessary.

3:19 pm

Before he got home, Rylan made a detour and stopped at one of the warehouses outside Solemnity Bay. On the warehouse above them, a giant cutout of a hammerhead shark swam menacingly like Rylan and Amos were plywood fish it was hunting for dinner. "SOLEMNITY BAY ADVENTURZ" was plastered above them in the kind of stylized font that always accompanied Ron Jons and Salt Water Souls. As Rylan pulled up, a wiry, slightly bow-legged man opened the door to the warehouse.

"Mike!" Rylan waved. There are two types of people who live in Solemnity Bay: people who enjoy the water, and people who make their living on the water. Mike Crenshaw was the latter. He wore faded denim and a ball cap with the ends coming undone, the kind of ball cap that used to be very popular but to him was a lifestyle choice. He made his living conducting shark tours and taking people out fishing for redfish.

"I didn't know Trekkies did that much shark hunting," Amos said to Rylan as he shook hands with Mike.

"Mike was my roommate at Tech for a year until he dropped out."

"Too much dirt up there, man," Mike said. "I needed some water, so I transferred to U of H and got my ME there. Been working boats and shark cages ever since. You ready to see it?"

"Sure."

The inside of the warehouse was like the inside of a forgotten tackle box where lines have spilled into separate trays and hooks have all left their bags. In the midst of the chaos sat several cages. The cage Mike pointed to had no bottom railing. It was barely big enough for a person to fit into, and unlike most shark cages, the door opened from the side instead of from the top.

"I left off the buoys and I welded the crossbars at two-foot intervals. I hope that makes it light enough for you to be able to carry."

"How much does it weigh?" Amos said.

"Lift it up yourself. It's aluminum."

It was surprisingly light. "It's tough, too. Bulls and Great Whites would have a hard fight getting into this cage."

"Will it protect him?"

Mike shrugged. "Let's be honest. It's built for sharks, not kaiju. I don't know how it will hold up against a monster that big. I haven't worked the physics out yet, but that's the adventure of it, right? After my boy survives, we'll have to work on the design further. But for now, check this out." He pointed to a small button welded to the interior of the cage.

"You push this button, and it fires four charges. Those charges will send bolts into the kaiju skin. Once those bolts hit, though, the only way out of the cage is through the door."

The door was small, barely wide enough for Rylan to fit through.

"Will you be able to fit through that?" Amos asked.

"It's amazing what you can squeeze through when the adrenaline's pumping through you," Mike said. Rylan agreed.

They loaded the cage into the truck, then thanked Mike and drove away. Mike followed them out in his Wrangler. He had been waiting to deliver the cage to Rylan before his evacuation. With a friendly wave and a honk, he turned west toward the sun. Rylan turned east toward Dolphin's Cove and the giant skeleton looming over his subdivision.

Amos checked messages on his phone. "Kaiju Gonzales' landfall has been upgraded to mid-day tomorrow."

"I thought kaiju preferred nighttime falls."

Amos shrugged. "Maybe the scavenger ones don't care. Is there anything I can do?"

He shook his head. "I need to put the drill together tonight and gather equipment for tomorrow."

3:48 pm

Rylan stood alone in Hiawatha's Garage. He pulled his weed eater off the wall and clamped it to his workbench. He discarded the attachments, then removed the engine from the body. There was a lot of work to do to modify the engine. He needed more power, and there wasn't much to gain on the 4-stroke engine. He started by taking his grinder to the exhaust port and widening it, then removing a little off the piston head. Then he upgraded the reed valve and replaced the air filter and fiddled with the timing. The timing took a while to perfect because he didn't want to overheat the piston. Once the timing was settled, he remixed the oil and gas. He used high-end oil and super-unleaded gasoline, but instead of using the recommended 40:1 ratio, he used half the oil. That risked the engine in the long term, but he only needed it to work for a day. He replaced the other half that was supposed to be oil with starting fluid.

When he revved the weed eaters engine, it made a powerful, high-pitched whine. He stopped for a sandwich and Coke, then put on his welding mask to create the necessary pipes and setup.

He finished the work before midnight, but a supercharged mixture of adrenaline and caffeine was keeping him awake. He was staring at the second turbocharger kit. Its sister was attached to the parasail. For Rylan's help, he was given the second turbocharger kit to keep. He looked back at the modified weed eater.

"Time to upsize."

By the time he was done, his weed whacker looked like something from a Mad Max movie that should shoot out flames.

What little sleep he got that night, he slept deeply. He dreamed of his wife and children.

+18 DAYS

5:39 am

The alarm went off before dawn, assaulting his ears with music from a local pop station. It was just what he needed. He hated pop music. Hearing One Direction or Ariana Grande was exactly the kind of thing that woke him up.

He thought of the slavering monster looming over his bed. But the monster was dead and he was alone, just him and his house. He jumped out of bed quickly. It was going to be a long day, so he might as well start early. He dressed like he was going to work at a rig: old jeans, work boots, cotton T-shirt, leather work gloves, industrial safety glasses, and a scraped-up hardhat with a Houston Dynamo sticker on the back.

He ate a quick breakfast and went out to the garage. There, the drillbit was loaded into a large backpack along with the other parts he needed. The pack and the shark cage were already in the truck bed. He got in the truck and said goodbye to Hiawatha's Garage and his house. In the solid dark of an unlit neighborhood, his lights shined on the thick painted lines zigzagging the street. Ainsley and Lisa had been very busy. He hoped their plan worked.

As he drove toward the kaiju grave, he noticed that some of the writings on the plywood coverings had crossed out Goliad for Gonzales.

Rylan thought on the quietude that had fallen over Dolphin's Cove. He guessed all but a crazy dozen had evacuated the area. Even the birds had evacuated. The flocks were all gone. Any animal in its right mind had gotten the hell out. "Solemnity Bay" seemed more appropriate a name for the town than it had probably been in centuries.

Ahead of him, a shallow stream of blood trickled out of Goliad. The kaiju's body had decomposed so much, the main road in and out of the Cove had been transformed into a bloody waterway. The odor was enough to knock him over. He coughed. It was bad. He pulled a bandana out from his glove compartment and put it over his mouth.

Goliad was a sludge of flesh and bodily fluid coalescing under a towering rib cage that may have finally stopped leaning in the direction of Rylan's house. He shined a flashlight up the rib. The beam dissipated before it could find the top of the ribs. Up there in the dark, NOAA had set up zip lines and belay lines for moving gear and personnel between the bones, and it was these lines that Rylan was going to appropriate for his use.

He pulled on the backpack with the drill bit and raised the shark cage over his shoulders. It was barely large enough to fit around him with his pack on. He then climbed over Goliad's skin and entered the beast's cavity. It was slippery inside, and he lost his footing more than once, sliding in the monster's fat, before he got to the belay line.

The rope seemed to go up forever and curl away into the sky. It was thin enough that from down on the ground he couldn't see exactly where it was bolted to the rib cage. He had looked a few days ago and seen that the line went almost to the very top. There would be a ledge that he would have to climb out onto, but otherwise, it was straight up to the ribcage. From ground level, though, the belay line gave the impression of one of those magical ropes that fakirs climbed.

He attached his self-belaying equipment and began the long climb to the top of Goliad's rib cage. As he climbed up into the darkness, he thought of the mantra to never look down. While he couldn't remember ever being prone to vertigo, he was not one to tempt it. However, after an hour of climbing, he had to look down to estimate his progress. In a weird way, he felt like he was back on the plains of Texas with no sense of distance or time.

Below him, his truck looked like a play car lying in the kaiju's shadow. Not two days ago, Goliad would have shrouded the area in a dark shadow until almost noon. Now, with much of his body reduced and eaten, morning light shined on the subdivision.

To the side, he could look out over his subdivision and all of Clear Lake. On the other side, he saw military personnel preparing for Gonzales' arrival. There was less than a third of the units he remembered seeing on television when Goliad made landfall. Most of the military probably was diverted to South Beach and the swarm. A single carrion kaiju whose intent was to eat remains, then return to the ocean? The only goal of the military in Solemnity Bay was to let Gonzales feast.

12:00 pm

Rylan reached the top of Goliad's ribcage. His arms had gone from feeling like fire to feeling like jelly, and his hamstrings were burning. He wished he had thought of his plan earlier so that he could have come up with lighter parts. He leaned back in his harness to rest while hanging in the air and enjoying the view. He could see from Galveston to downtown Houston from the top of the ribs. The sun was up and the smog had dissipated; he could see the Galleria. People there were buying Armani shirts for their kids and gawking at Teslas. In ten years, those same people would probably be paying to zip down lines across Goliad's bones just like Rylan was doing now. It didn't make them bad people, and it didn't make him better than them, but the thought was there in his head all the same.

There were steps drilled into the vertebra where agents could reach down and lift equipment and personnel as needed. Getting up on his own, however, would be much more difficult. He ate a granola bar and drank from his canteen, then wiped the sweat from his brow. A minute later, he used what was left of his strength to pull himself up over the rib bone. His arms shook as he hefted himself up. His arms wanted to give up on him, and for a second he thought that he would not get up on the vertebra, that he had done all this work to turn himself into an easy target for Gonzales. Then in one motion, he was up and on top of the rib. Arms and legs flopped over the side of the rib, dangling in the air. He didn't care. He lay there on his stomach, pressed into his own shark cage under the risen sun. Beads of sweat dripped from his brow and fell down towards Buzzards circling in the sky below him, then disappeared.

Sirens wailed.

Rylan crawled to his feet. The murky waters of the bay moved in its usual lackadaisical languor. Seagulls flew over an inlet devastated by Goliad's entry. They dove at the shimmering line of fish that once again found themselves caught between predators. Then suddenly a gigantic switchblade claw like the front leg of a praying mantis shot out of the water and crashed on land. While Rylan sat in awe of a claw so big it defied description, a second claw shot out of the water and raked into the ground, destroying a small house. Then the claws pulled a hideous face, wide and flat, out of the bay. Giant waterfalls of bay water cascaded off of the kaiju's head.

The scale of the monster was unbelievable. It was there before him, and he still didn't believe it. He was looking at his first kaiju up close and in person, and it was bigger than anything engineered by man. It was colossal. It was gigantic. Hell, its size was beyond words. Gonzales was Big Tex riding a jumbotron-sized Bevo through Jerryworld. It just didn't get bigger than this.

Four additional legs rose up out of the bay. How does it support the weight, the engineer in him wondered. Its upright body was covered in tall spikes. Good, Rylan thought. The spikes give me a hiding place. Rylan had to remind himself that this was the "small" kaiju. The large one lay below him.

The kaiju looked around as if searching for predators, then stepped out onto homes. The military stood their ground, having created a path for the scavenger kaiju to approach the kaiju fall.

"Come on," Rylan said. "Come and take it."

When Gonzales bellowed, it was like a hurricane gale that sent him sliding off into the never. Thankfully, he was still buckled, so when his body dropped over the side, the belay caught him. The cage popped against him, and he lost his hardhat. As it fell, the bright orange Dynamo shield seemed to blink as the hardhat flipped and sailed down into Kaiju Goliad's guts.

He felt like a tiny St. George waiting for a very extraordinary dragon. He did not remember much of the legend of St. George and the dragon, but he remembered something about sacrifices to the dragon, which did not help him feel better. He was not a very religious man, but he made the sign of the cross.

While Rylan dangled like a tiny spec of gunk on the end of an unwashed hair, Kaiju Gonzales crossed 146. Soldiers crouched with rocket launchers and automatic rifles aimed at a monster impervious to their weapons. They hoped the kaiju would not veer from her course. The reality was they could do little to deter it. Sure, bring in enough bombs and a kaiju could be encouraged to leave, or get lucky and slice open its underside, but most kaiju just had to run their course until they fell down and died. With any luck, they landed in a vacant stretch of land or never made it to shore.

Unfortunately, every kaiju was different. No one species had been discovered yet, which made them as much a mystery as where they came from. Even the carrion ones were different, but at least they could be grouped together in a class. Some carrion eaters were more vulpine like Kaiju Vicksburg, and others were more like crab-walkers, but Kaiju Gonzales stood up on her back four and was covered in spikes and had a wide, gaping mouth.

Kaiju Gonzales stopped on the near side of 146, just steps away from Goliad. She sniffed the air, then looked north and south, again, as if sensing for a predator. Then she opened her wide mouth and bit down on Goliad's carcass. She shook the meat, which ripped, then flung her head back as she gulped it down. Rylan remembered the skin being hard as packed concrete, and wondered how much force was needed to rip apart a kaiju.

Rylan reached up to the steps that were punched into the rib bone. He let his arms hang from the steps for a second, then pulled. But as soon as he felt his weight on his arms, he knew he didn't have the strength to pull him and his pack of gear back up on the rib. Maybe, if he pushed himself harder than ever, he could get up on the rib, but to what end? He was leaving it no matter what. He might as well save his strength for the kaiju.

He waited, and the soldiers waited, and Kaiju Gonzales took another bite out of Goliad's hide. Rylan needed Gonzales to come closer so he could fall on him. The expanse between them now was too great for him to do anything. He was as useful as a pen and paper for somebody without an idea.

Gonzales hunched down and entered Goliad's ribcage. Rylan hadn't thought much of the difference in size between the two monsters, but now he thought back to the difference in how they appeared on Doppler radars, how Goliad had been like a long line and Gonzales was more like a blip. It reminded him of something a NASA engineer friend of his said once of visiting Kennedy Space Center, back before the Space Shuttle Program shut down.

"It's a mind-blowing experience of scale and size," she had said. "First you see the crawler, and you think it is the biggest thing ever. I mean, it's a two-story car almost the size of half a football field! But then you go up in the Vehicle Assembly Building, and you are looking down at those rocket boosters, and the world seems so small down there. You are high enough – inside a building – for clouds to gather. That's insane. Then you visit the launch pad, which holds all of that technology, and the rocket booster is only one component of the whole system, and the crawler – something you saw earlier that day and could not believe how big it was – is now a tiny little pad that holds up everything else. It's something you have to see to believe."

One epically-sized kaiju inside the ribcage of another. It, too, was something you had to see to believe. It was another reminder of how little they knew about these monsters and where they came from. Expeditions had been held, but nobody had yet to enter the trench and come back alive.

Right now, dangling from a belay line hooked to Kaiju Goliad's rib cage, Rylan just wanted this new monster out of his neighborhood and away from his house.

Kaiju Gonzales finished tearing at Goliad's skin. The gargantuan beast stepped inside Kaiju Goliad's cavity and looked at him with giant, slitted eyes. One breath, one bite, was all it took to end Rylan's life. She licked her lips while she considered the human mote the way a dog considers an ant.

But then the kaiju lowered herself to eat. She was now below him. It was time to release himself from the belay and turn his life over to physics. He had to do a weird thing first. It wasn't enough to simply let go. He had to pull himself up to cut the tension on the belay device. It was symbolic of the choice he was making to ride the kaiju and try to force her out.

He took a breath. Thought of his wife and children and reminded himself that he was where he wanted to be. This was the choice he made. Nobody had forced him to do this. It was like with his wife. He had to go find her after insulting her the first time they met. It was a conscious decision on his part, just like it was his choice to marry her. Everything in his life was a string of choices that put him here in this exact moment and space.

As a child, he had chosen to go to that after-school STEM class. He chose to join the robotics leagues. He chose to go to Texas Tech instead of the University of Houston, where most of his friends went to school. And when he graduated, he had three offers from three different companies. Shell Oil, Haliburton, and Tatanka Oil. He chose Tatanka Oil. Who knows what would have happened if he had chosen Shell or the University of Houston or to not join the engineering club? Would he have still decided to come back to Houston to rebuild his home after Kaiju Goliad's attack? Would he have attacked the parasite or moved the kaiju egg or concocted this crazy idea to detour Kaiju Gonzales away from his home? He had made many important decisions over the past week, but none so important as letting go of the belay line.

Light streamed around the giant spikes of Kaiju Gonzales.

Rylan pulled himself up, then released his grip on the rope.

He was airborne. He was a slave to gravity.

The spikes moved. The beast was turning away from him. And he had no control over what happened next.

Gonzales was rising up. As he was falling, the beast was rising. It would hit him like a ton of concrete. He doubted that the shark cage would provide more protection than a cage made of paperclips.

And then he struck a spike and was rolling along it like a satellite lander trying to find purchase on a trailing comet. Rylan was scrambling, reaching for anything that would offer him a grasp. But Kaiju Gonzales' skin was wet and slippery; water still fell from her body. His only hope was to grab hold of the tiny nubs and ridges in the monster's skin that flashed past him, or ahead of him. He wasn't sure which. Direction was lost to him. He began to tumble along a spike. Then the cage hit something and his body was jerked to the side. He didn't know where he was anymore. He just grabbed. Grabbed and prayed.

12:07 pm

A moment later, he dared to open his eyes. He was caught between several gigantic spikes on Goliad's back. He was pressed against his cage, which was wedged between the spikes.

He felt more than heard the monster gulping down a chunk of Goliad's flesh. The meal passed down Gonzales's throat, pushing a ripple through her body. He realized then just how lucky he had been. That Kaiju Gonzales was rising up to gulp while Rylan had been falling. He had miscalculated his distance and would have fallen much farther had she not risen up to meet him. He had bounced around the spikes like a pinball and was now resting somewhere on Kaiju Gonzales' back. Where, exactly, was not obvious. He was surrounded by three giant spikes the color of purple iron. They hid the rest of Kaiju Gonzales from his view.

Between the spikes, though, he could see Clear Lake and the Houston skyline. It was a weird view, to say the least. If he had thought to bring his camera, he probably would have broken the internet if he tweeted a picture of his view. He would just have to settle for breaking a kaiju.

First things first, he thought. He unwedged the shark cage and leveled it against the kaiju's back. Of the cage's four legs, only one was crooked and beyond repair. He pressed the button Mike had installed, and the cartridges exploded. It was a muffled sound as the bolts slammed into Kaiju Gonzales' thick hide. When it was done, he was latched to the creature's body. He couldn't be shook off or blown off. He was like a horsefly that wouldn't leave.

He reached behind him and pulled the drillbit out of his pack, then placed the piece of machinery against the kaiju's flesh. The bit fit into a small shaft with its own bolts, which he had rigged together last night. Most importantly, the shaft had a kickstand so that he could put weight on the drill bit. All the parts he had carefully placed in his pack. The drill bit was now ready to dig. He reached behind him and pulled the cord on the edger. The little engine roared to life with a power blessed by the gods of innovation. He adjusted his safety goggles and held out the shaft. He pulled a thin metal tube from the backpack. It was maybe three feet long. Once it clicked into place in the drill bit, he pulled out another and clicked it into place. The spike was centered in front of his head. Everything was ready. He pressed the button to start the engine and stood on the kickstand. The drill bit sent up sparks, showering Rylan in gold and silver fury. He had to push hard to keep the drill bit from kicking out from under him, so he propped himself against the cage and hoped that his buddy from college who sometimes still smoked weed did his best work on the cage. Hopefully despite missing one leg of the cage, it would still hold him and the drill bit down.

Elsewhere, giant Gonzales pushed aside more flesh and dined on Goliad's inner cavity until her face and claws were stained red with blood. She was oblivious to the little man boring a tiny hole in her long back. She turned in the ribcage and consumed what was left of Goliad's long-dead heart.

The shower-spray of sparks had died down as the drill bit disappeared into her skin. This was the hard part, he knew. Once the drill had passed ten feet, max, then it would be inside the kaiju's cavity and wrecking true destruction. If he was lucky and kaiju anatomy was anything like most Earth creatures (and he had to believe the anatomy was similar because what point was there to drilling into the kaiju's gallbladder?), he was drilling towards the monster's heart. At least, he was drilling toward a lung. Both could be mortal wounds to the giant monster. Could be. He was no expert in biology, so he didn't know how deep a hole he had to drill into a kaiju's heart or lung to make it collapse. If he was unlucky, he would hit bone. If that happened, he had no way of gauging the increase of pressure except to visually judge the rise and fall of the drill bit by the movement of the poles he was inserting into the shaft. It was like unclogging a toilet and not knowing whether the auger was entering the toilet's pipeline or was stuck on a twist.

By then, Kaiju Gonzales had moved again. Every time the beast moved, Rylan's ears popped from the change in air pressure. It was like trying to drill on a roller coaster. If not for the shark cage being bolted to the skin, he would have fallen off long ago, like a bull rider trying to make 8 seconds on the back of the world's surliest bull. Currently, he was drilling at a forty five degree angle. His feet were propped against the back rails of the cage.

12:38 pm

The drilling was slower than he wanted, but he didn't exactly have the usual drilling motors employed in his industry. So far, the piston seemed to be working well, and the parasail turbocharger was doing its job. At least the kaiju was content with gorging on Goliad, which meant she was steady and not bouncing around so much.

Rylan pushed a third pipe into the shaft. As it clicked into place and started rotating, he felt the pressure building up again as the drill bit began kicking. He thought heat pressure could be causing the drill to kick. At the rigs, they poured different "muds" into the holes to reduce pressure and help maintain a drill. But with his pack already close to a hundred pounds, he knew he had no room or strength to carry another fifty pounds of mud.

He grabbed a water bottle and poured it into the hole. With any luck, some of the salt water still pouring off Gonzales' body would dump into the hole and help keep it cool. It might rust out the drill bit, but long-term maintenance of his equipment wasn't one of his concerns; he just hoped to survive the next thirty minutes.

The drill bit with its goblin shark mouth of circulating teeth kept digging into Kaiju Gonzales.

Behind him, one of the giant purple/black spikes split open, exposing a very pink and fleshy underside full of pink tentacles. The tentacles searched for the assailant like the hungry hands of blind men dying of old age.

Rylan, oblivious, stopped the drill to load a fourth pole. He took the chance to look down into his hole. He did not have a flashlight to tell him how well the drill was working, but he knew he must be close to breaching the skin. He started getting the engineer's rush, which was the thrill of building equipment and then seeing it work successfully in the field. Until it works in the field, it is either in design or it is in review. But here on the back of the kaiju, his clothes soaked in brine and sweat, the drill was working. Some things had to be forged in the fire. It was unexplored territory, which made him happy in a way that only people like Shackleton and Edison could understand. He had a chance to do something nobody had ever done before, which was single-handedly kill a kaiju. Instead of Bring Em Back Alive, it was Take Them Out Dead.

He pressed the ignition and thought of the possibilities. After Kaiju Gonzales fell, he could sell his design to the military. He'd make a fortune, which would be good because Tatanka would probably fire him for stealing a $500 drill bit. Then again, once he used it to bring down a titan like this, maybe they wouldn't be so quick to judge. He was just being the petro engineer they hired him to be. Finding technical solutions to the world's problems.

That's when the tentacles wrapped around his arms and legs.

"What the hell?" He pulled his pocket knife out, but before he could unfold the saw blade, a tentacle knocked it out of his hand. The knife went flying down the side of the kaiju and out into oblivion. The tentacle found Rylan's arm and curled around it like long fingers. Once it had him, the pink flesh was like a vise. It pulled him away from the hole and toward the spike. Rylan saw little hooked teeth embedded in the flesh. He thought of the mass that had landed in his children's Secret Room. How long had he been around that thing? He and his neighbors had cut its tentacles then and never saw teeth. Was it not mature enough? Were the teeth only activated once the male came into contact with the female? There was still so little he understood about the kaiju.

Right now, in this moment, what mattered was staying alive. The shark cage was keeping him alive. The tentacles could not pull him through, though they were trying. The pressure was painful. Where the tentacle grabbed his upper arm, his skin was turning white and his fingers were tingling. He knew the tentacles cut easily, but he had no way to cut them. Besides the pocket knife, there was only one other cutting device.

He scrambled to pull pipes out of the drill hole and expunge his bit. It was hard to do with one hand. Pipes went flying. His captured arm felt like it was going to snap under the pressure.

More tentacles reached for the cage and tried to rip it off of the kaiju's skin. The last tentacle reached out and grabbed his right leg. Rylan stiffened his leg. There was a little hole in the cage from the broken post, which was bent outward. The tentacle was trying to pull Rylan out through the tiny hole.

Rylan fell to one knee as the tentacle pulled his foot out of the hole and toward the hook-like teeth. The drill bit finally came out of the hole. He twisted and let the bit fall towards the spike as he turned the engine on. The drill went into the spike like a tiller through soft flesh. Tentacles immediately let go and began to shake and wither as the spike screamed its death rattle.

Tentacles were not coming from the other spikes. Either they had learned the lesson, or they were incapable of sprouting tentacles.

Rylan shook sensation back into his hand while he pulled the drill bit back to him, reeling it in like a fish, and placed it back into the hole. He attached two of the four pipes he could find, then fished two more pipes out of his backpack. He hoped he had enough. He had done some serious math to come up with the numbers he believed he needed to get through Gonzales' heart. He of course took into consideration some breaking, but every pipe he knew would be more weight to carry, so he only gave himself three spares.

He pushed the fourth rod into the shaft and pressed the button to start the drill back up.

12:49 pm

Beyond Rylan, Gonzales pushed out Goliad's ribcage and licked her massive lips. Blood and gore dribbled from her wide mouth, which was bearded with shortened tentacles. She leaned into a step as she was about to walk around the western side of Goliad, but then hesitated. Her inset eyes studied the striped shape on the ground for a moment. She scanned the horizon once more, then ducked back inside the rib cage, which was mostly bone. She began working her way down to Goliad's tail, supping up entrails larger than train lines.

She stopped suddenly and rolled her shoulders. Then she shook her body. The shaking sounded like a windstorm. Military personnel on the ground, and a few circling her in Blackhawks that stayed outside a 200 meter range, waited for Gonzales' next move.

On her back, Rylan gripped the bars and held on for dear life. He was sure the cage was going to spin off at any second. He had let go of the drill once Kaiju Gonzales began to shake. A moment before, blood burst out of his pipeline like oil gushing from a wildcatter's derrick. He had finally breached the thick outer skin. Then Kaiju Gonzales began shaking, and he grabbed his head. He was worried about hitting the bars. There was enough force to split his head open like a Texas grapefruit. She stopped shaking, and he took inventory of his damage. His arms were bruised, and there was a knot on his head with an open sore, but he had survived.

He was also thoroughly and completely soaked in kaiju blood. At least it's not sweat, he thought.

He had affected her. Like a fire ant's bit, he had hurt her in a way that she moved. This was something. Encouraged, he wiped his gloves off on the kaiju's skin and began drilling again. He thrust another pipe into the hole. The blood stopped gushing, which he expected. He had breached the outer skin, not organ.

He had her. He just had to keep going.

Suddenly the sky went dark around him like it does when a storm rises up off the horizon. A giant claw appeared in the sky, reaching for him. It snapped back when it couldn't get through the spikes, then reached out again, stretching like the open jaws of a snapping turtle trying to pluck him up. There would be no stopping that claw if it got him. It would squash him like the insignificant bug he was. He thought of his children and his wife and ducked closer to the skin.

The upside of being such a small insect on such a large body was that he had landed in that sweet spot that just can't be scratched, especially when your body is covered in giant male adornments. She could not reach him. No matter how hard she tried, the claws could get no closer than five feet to him.

Rylan jammed another pipe into the hole. Now the blood was really gushing. The problem now was that the pressure rising from the blood stream was preventing the drill from pushing deeper into her body. This was a good problem as far as Rylan was concerned.

And then he was upside down and from above him came a giant piece of bone: Goliad's rib. At this point, Rylan was slipping and had lost total control of the drill. He was sitting on the ceiling of the shark cage while kaiju bone collapsed on him like the falling ceiling in an Indiana Jones movie. The rib pushed down farther and farther, pushing aside the ends of the spikes. A few feet from him, the rib finally got wedged between the spikes. Dust and debris kicked up by the kaiju fall suffocated the air. He was glad for the bandana.

Then out of his dusty view, the vertebra fell away from him. He felt like he was in one of those drop zone amusement rides, the one where the carriage is taken to the top of a pole and then dropped several times before finally coming to a rest at the bottom, only to then feel your stomach sink to your knees as the carriage is pulled back up again.

Again came the crushing blow, and again he was slammed within feet of the vertebra. This time he was so close that if he reached out with his hand, he could feel the indentations in the vertebra.

The world tumbled over and over, and he nearly lost his stomach as he again hid his head in his arms. But when Gonzales finished, he was back upright with his feet braced against the cage and the drill still in the hole. He reached for the next pipe. Three, maybe four more pipes, and he would have this monster.

There was only one pipe left. The others had spilled out while Gonzales shook, or maybe when Gonzales tried to squash him into the vertebra. He had only three feet more he could dig. .

As the world started to swirl around him again, Rylan clicked the pipe into place and pulled the cord on his modified weed whacker. He thanked God that the engine hadn't failed him yet. He stepped onto the stand and braced his body into the cage as the drill pushed deeper into the kaiju's core. Blood spewed out of the hole as the kaiju's body shook.

"C'mon," he urged his equipment. The last pipe came flush against the skin. He arched his back and stretched to try to push it deeper into the kaiju. The engine sputtered. He could smell the oil burning outside the piston. Apparently, being turned upside down over and over again and slammed into a vertebra was wrecking havoc on the fluids in the engine, and now they were leaking out.

He thought of leaving, then. He had done all he could. Dug the hole as deep as it would go. If it didn't hit its mark, it didn't hit its mark. It wasn't like he had a supplier he could go to for more equipment or like he could go to a trailer and analyze the data over some coffee and kolaches while trying to figure out a new way to get at the heart.

His wife's words came to him. She hadn't asked him to leave if things go to hell. She had said, please, three times, for him to get out of there if things go to hell. Well, he was in the proverbial hand basket. For a half-second, he wondered where the idiom came from. What is hell in a hand basket? Was somebody carrying around a hand basket full of dynamite, or plague? Who was the first person to use this phrase, and why did they choose to use it? Surely, the alliteration gave a nice ring to it. But he had no clue where the phrase "hell in a hand basket" came from. Maybe it was coined in war. War is hell, so why can't it be hell in a hand basket? He did not know. This was hell in a hand basket. And when he survived this adventure and saved his house, he wanted to find out where the phrase came from.

"I'll give you hell in a hand basket," he yelled at Gonzales. It sounded stupid coming out of his mouth. Nobody could hear him, though, except maybe the kaiju, and she had no concern for his declaration.

He pushed down harder on the stand. The pipe had not disappeared yet, but it was still spinning in the hole. If he was lucky, it might break through the lung.

He yelled and screamed against the rain of blood and the churning world. And then, the flesh broke. He felt the pop in his bones, and then currents of dark blood gushed over and around him, and he had a hard time breathing in the flood.

The current pulsed, and he knew he had done some sinister damage. The kind of damage you don't escape alive. Gonzales was bleeding out.

As part of the next current, the pipe shot out of the hole, cutting a gash in his chin, and twisting in the cage. Rylan had to move to the side to not be trapped by the pipe. Then the current gushed again, and the world rolled on him, and the pipe bent into the cage. Rylan needed an exit strategy, and he needed one quick.

He stripped off his pack and tried to climb out of the cage through the door. But the next pulse bent the pipe more. Twisted pipe was between him and the door. He was trapped in the shark cage. He had to kneel because the pipe was now taking up most of the space in the top half of the cage.

He leaned down and checked the hole in the bottom of the cage. Could his bad luck from earlier in the battle be his savior? But there was no way to fit through the hole, even when fully lubricated in kaiju blood. He tested the bars, but if they were strong enough to deter a shark attack, they were stronger than him.

The bolts, however, were another thing. They were designed for rock, not flesh, and so were starting to give way to the pressure from the pipe pushing against the cage. The bolts had risen one to two inches out of the kaiju's skin. They would only hold for so long. Each current of blood increased the likelihood that the cage would break from its grasp of the kaiju. And what then?

Was his house worth this? Even if he had been behind payments on a double-mortgage and facing bankruptcy, which he wasn't – would it have been worth dying over? Rylan wondered if he was that different from his neighbor who was draped in a tarp on his driveway.

He decided there were three deaths he was facing. He could stay where he was and be crushed by the pipe that was filling up the hole. If the drill bit escaped the hole, he could also be killed by the flying teeth. And if the cage broke free, he would fall to his death. There was no way of knowing where he was or where he would land. All he saw was a moving island of kaiju spikes set against a backdrop of blue sky. He had no idea how high up he was or where he was. For all he knew, he could be in downtown Houston, Kaiju Gonzales stomping through the skyscrapers. He felt like he was riding bareback on a hurricane.

Maybe this was what Pecos Bill felt like when he rode a twister across Texas, Rylan thought in a moment of levity. Of course, that was a tall tale. This is a mother fucking kaiju.

Only one of those death options gave him choice. Maybe he could slide down the kaiju's back, or maybe he would get lucky and survive a fall to the ground. He had heard of people who survived parachute drops after the parachute failed to deploy. So there was a chance there. But staying in the cage was accepting death, and he had a wife and two sons.

He reached under the bars and pulled as hard as he could. He heard the cage groan, and then a pipe pounded him in the shoulder. How much more pipe could come out before he was locked in a cage with a flying mouth full of metal teeth? He readjusted his body and strained again.

From not as far away as he'd like, the monster roared, but in Rylan's head, he heard the growl of the tornado that wiped away his family's home.

Then a wave of water pulverized him.

From his little spot tucked away on Kaiju Gonzales' back, he had not seen the kaiju running for the water. He felt his stomach lurch as the kaiju jumped into the water, but his stomach had been experiencing a strange form of seasickness ever since climbing on top of the kaiju. The movement of the beast translated to a single human mote was incomprehensible to Rylan. He was like an anole trapped on the hood of an 18-wheeler, not knowing where it was going or what it was experiencing.

So when the beast crashed into the Gulf of Mexico, his knees buckled, but his eyes were closed as he strained against the bars. He did not see the giant wave rising up like some horror movie's special effect. But when Kaiju Gonzales dove underneath and the water came crashing back inward over his back, Rylan felt that. If not for the cage, he would have been smashed among the kaiju's spikes. But now, he was trapped in a cage underwater without a breathing apparatus.

The pipe continued to snake around the cage, buckling and twisting like a snake thrown on a fire pit.

Rylan was not a swimmer. He gave himself maybe thirty seconds before he would stop struggling and just writhe until he either gulped down water or lost consciousness.

Finally, the cage gave way. The cage separated from the kaiju, and Rylan rolled in the monster's wake. When he finally stopped rolling and gained some sense of direction, he started swimming to the surface. But not before he saw the massive kaiju turn around and stare at him. A chill gushed up from the base of his spine and exploded throughout his body. He forgot about drowning and stayed there motionless. Gonzales watched him with a mouth wider than a supermarket. The mouth opened far enough to show Rylan all those rows of teeth that were more like stalagmites jutting from the base of the jaw than individual teeth.

He waited for the inevitable charge of the kaiju or the quick snap that would end his life. Whether he lived or died was no longer his choice. It was the choice of Kaiju Gonzales. This, almost more than anything else, was what scared him. He had been robbed of his choices. No decision he made could alter the outcome of his life. Then the kaiju turned and swam away. She glared at him, first. It was the glare of his granny sparing the rod this time mixed with the glare of a tiger that wants you to know you are utterly, unbelievably inferior. The point was clear: I can kill you. Whether she was too pained or too full from devouring most of the meat left on Goliad, Rylan did not know. He did not wait to find out what happened to her. He rose up through the salty water and gasped for air. All around him was water and waves.

+20 DAYS

1:15 pm

Blackhawks following Kaiju Gonzales picked Rylan up in the Gulf of Mexico, almost a mile off shore. They were not equipped for water rescue, but like the greatest military minds, they improvised. A soldier rappelled down to him, and others pulled them up into the helicopter. Rylan was awake for all of this.

"You are the dumbest son of a bitch I have ever seen," the soldier said.

Rylan never picked up the soldier's name, and didn't remember what he said to him, either. He fell asleep from exhaustion and woke up two days later in the hospital surrounded by his family. Tamara cried in joy. She gently wrapped her arms around his head, careful not to touch any of the stitches, and kissed him on the lips.

"I missed you," she said softly.

"I'm sorry. I didn't mean…"

She shushed him and kissed him again. Then his boys came rushing up.

"Don't you jump on your daddy!"

Rylan's finger was wrapped in gauze, but he still reached out to them. After they finished hugging, he asked Tamara, "When did I break my finger?"

"There's a lot you don't know," she said.

"Daddy, you were on TV!" James and John Clayton shouted.

"Was I?"

"People are calling you a hero!"

"I don't think…" he started to say, but James interrupted.

"Bill O'Reilly says you're an idiot."

"Well, we don't care what Mr. O'Reilly says," Tamara told James. "We are just glad our daddy is back, right boys?"

As the kids cheered, she said, "And daddy is never EVER going to do something like that again, is he?"

"No!" the boys shouted jubilantly.

"Mommy says we get ice cream if we waited nicely for you to come out of your medically induced coma."

The doctors he hadn't really seen were around him then. They told him he had suffered a moderate Traumatic Brain Injury, or TBI, and was placed in a medically induced coma. Now that he had shown improvement, they had taken him out of the coma and wanted to run some tests. They checked his blood pressure and pupil dilation and had him answer a few questions. His head still hurt, but it was less of a headache and more of a stitches-in-the-head matter. His vision felt fine and words were coming easily to him. He didn't remember anything from the last two days, however.

"When you were pulled from the water, you fell unconscious. You woke up in the hospital, but your speech was slurred. An MRI showed swelling in your brain, so it was decided to put you in a medically induced coma to reduce swelling. You are lucky to be alive."

He held his hand up and looked to Tamara, who was sitting in the corner. James and John Clayton were in the waiting room with their uncle. The doctor stopped talking.

"I have to know what happened to our house."

She smiled and nodded. He leaned back into the bed and absorbed the good news. Then he let the doctor continue his line of questions.

Later that day, they ran a second MRI on him. He was also up and walking and moving his arms, though tired.

"I guess I used up all my energy on the kaiju."

"Just shut up and sit down," Tamara said.

+25 DAYS

Twenty five days after Goliad made landfall, his family returned home.

He had learned what had happened while he was bull riding the kaiju across South Houston. After he hit an organ, which is now believed to be the heart, the kaiju tried rolling to get him off. When that didn't work, it tried to squash him on Goliad's sternum. Rylan remembered that moment when he could reach out and touch the bone. In that brief moment, he had felt like an astronaut on an alien world touching an alien planet.

When that failed, Kaiju Gonazles went back to open water. But instead of returning to the bay, she ran to Galveston and launched herself into the Gulf of Mexico. She swam away then, but died before making it back to the trench. Her body fell to the floor of the Gulf of Mexico, turning the carrion-eater into carrion for fish.

His home was cleaned up by his neighbors, who were all there to see him. The outside of Dolphin's Cove still looked like a warzone, though maybe a little less so. Some of the roads were being repaired. His lawn was mowed and the roof repaired. The gutters were all replaced and the outside of the house had been repainted. It looked better than he ever remembered it.

A dozen or two news crews were surrounding the house when they drove up. Tamara was driving the Silverado, of course. Balloons were tied to lawn stakes, and signs of well-wishes and flowers had been planted. All his neighbors were there in the driveway as they drove up, including Lisa and Ainsley, Jim and Christine, and Amos. Even the neighbors he didn't know were there. (He was pretty sure some of the people didn't even belong in the subdivision, which was kind of ironic to him after all those days playing hide-and-seek with the police.)

Rylan shook hands with the people he remembered from the stand-off with the gang in his backyard. For Lisa, Ainsley, Amos, Jim, and Christine, however, he gave hugs. He waved to the crowd, thanked them for their support, and then went inside with his family. Tamara led them in a prayer, and then the boys found their gamepads and tablets. The boys ran upstairs and into their Secret Rooms.

"Is that safe?" he asked.

"Insurance works fast when you're in the middle of your fifteen minutes of fame. So remember to wave to the camera and thank All State."

He walked around the house, hand-in-hand with his wife, and he examined all the repaired damage.

"The insurance company replaced the furniture and everything?"

"Oh, some of it was donated. Others were just people being kind. Many of your neighbors helped out. Jim donated a new set of knives. Said you would find that funny."

"I do."

He kissed his wife.

Thanks for Reading

Kaiju Fall is a story of the real struggles that begin after a kaiju is killed. If you enjoyed the book, please leave a review on Amazon. These reviews not only help others pick books, but also help authors to be seen. Doug Goodman is also the author of a post-apocalyptic thriller, Dominion, (also out from Severed Press) and a collection of bloody Arthurian Tales, Warriors of Camlann.
His books can be found at:
http://www.amazon.com/Doug-Goodman/e/B00IHF1I8S/ref=dp_byline_cont_pop_ebooks_1
As always, his website is www.douggoodman.net.

 SEVERED**PRESS**

 facebook.com/severedpress
 twitter.com/severedpress

CHECK OUT OTHER GREAT
KAIJU NOVELS

MURDER WORLD I KAIJU DAWN
by Jason Cordova
& Eric S Brown

Captain Vincente Huerta and the crew of the Fancy have been hired to retrieve a valuable item from a downed research vessel at the edge of the enemy's space.
It was going to be an easy payday.
But what Captain Huerta and the men, women and alien under his command didn't know was that they were being sent to the most dangerous planet in the galaxy.
Something large, ancient and most assuredly evil resides on the planet of Gorgon IV. Something so terrifying that man could barely fathom it with his puny mind. Captain Huerta must use every trick in the book, and possibly write an entirely new one, if he wants to escape Murder World.

KAIJU ARMAGEDDON
by Eric S. Brown

The attacks began without warning. Civilian and Military vessels alike simply vanished upon the waves. Crypto-zoologist Jerry Bryson found himself swept up into the chaos as the world discovered that the legendary beasts known as Kaiju are very real. Armies of the great beasts arose from the oceans and burrowed their way free of the Earth to declare war upon mankind. Now Dr. Bryson may be the human race's last hope in stopping the Kaiju from bringing civilization to its knees.
This is not some far distant future. This is not some alien world. This is the Earth, here and now, as we know it today, faced with the greatest threat its ever known. The Kaiju Armageddon has begun.

CHECK OUT OTHER GREAT KAIJU NOVELS

KAIJU WINTER
by Jake Bible

The Yellowstone super volcano has begun to erupt, sending North America into chaos and the rest of the world into panic. People are dangerous and desperate to escape the oncoming mega-eruption, knowing it will plunge the continent, and the world, into a perpetual ashen winter. But no matter how ready humanity is, nothing can prepare them for what comes out of the ash: Kaiju!

RAIJU
by K.H. Koehler

His home destroyed by a rampaging kaiju, Kevin Takahashi and his father relocate to New York City where Kevin hopes the nightmare is over. Soon after his arrival in the Big Apple, a new kaiju emerges. Qilin is so powerful that even the U.S. Military may be unable to contain or destroy the monster. But Kevin is more than a ragged refugee from the now defunct city of San Francisco. He's also a Keeper who can summon ancient, demonic god-beasts to do battle for him, and his creature to call is Raiju, the oldest of the ancient Kami. Kevin has only a short time to save the city of New York. Because Raiju and Qilin are about to clash, and after the dust settles, there may be no home left for any of them!